THE METHODS OF
TALENT
AND
POTENTIAL
2

A Rivalry Amongst Relatives

by MARQUIS "POOH" DUNN

The Methods of Talent and Potential 2

Pres.tig.ious Publications

Copyright 2023 by Marquis "Pooh" Dunn

Dedications

I dedicate this book to every little inner-city child throughout the country who's been written off, not considered, discarded, looked down upon, or viewed as valueless in the eyes of society. Just know that we can never give up on ourselves nor can we fully listen to the negative opinions of others. Because God is always in control.

In loving memory of my Big Brother Carlos Franklin and my two childhood best friends, you will forever be missed and always remembered my brothers, rest peacefully.

Acknowledgements

As always, I would like to thank God, for making this all possible, and for giving me the ability to create another story, in which I believe is a little different from the previous, but still magnifies Him {God} in ways that I am extremely proud of.

I also want to thank God, for everyone who not only supported me in the writing of my first book, but who also expressed to me their feelings, thoughts, concerns, beliefs, enjoyments, or things that were sort of misunderstood. This gave me the ability to have open discussions with them and we were all enlightened in one way or another. Thank you so much.

Finally, I would like to thank my family, both living and deceased, because you all have continually made this the most fun for me to do, especially my mother, children, and grandchildren.

When I'm Speaking of family, I am not just referring to all of my relatives, but also my extremely close friends, those that have stood closer to me than a brother or sister as Proverbs 18:24 speaks about.

Whether bound or free, both living and deceased, doesn't make any difference to me. I love you regardless! Tee, we've done it again homie!

Shout out to all my incarcerated black men and women across the nation. My prayers go out to you all... And that's real! God bless you because God has not forgotten you...

Marquis "Pooh" Dunn

Introduction

Bullets have flown, and more lies have been told while deception, deceit, and betrayal is at an all-time high amongst the Clifton and McCreary families, creating completely new enemies, while manifesting the intensity of their previous foes to the 3rd degree. Both families try to hold it all together by constantly relying on God's strength but steadily seeming to lose their grip as the devil's many conniving and cunning tactics appear to be dismantling both the Clifton's and the McCreary's armor.

Especially Talent and Potential's, who now appear to be in the fight of their lives in order to protect their souls, as Liz amongst many others repetitiously attack their faith and beliefs with a vengeance.

THE METHODS OF
TALENT
AND
POTENTIAL
2

A Rivalry Amongst Relatives

Prologue

The building was as big as The Parthenon of Centennial Park and constructed with the same type of style and elegance.

Big John couldn't wait to step foot inside of it. Although he had dropped out of school at an early age himself, Big John never lost the passion for reading and learning about the heritage of his people and couldn't wait to pass his knowledge along to one of the only other male members of the Clifton family, his grandson Potential, whom he instantly pulled closer to him as they both entered the building.

The marbled floors were waxed and polished like that of a ballroom's dance hall. As each of the Clifton's reflections vividly shone back at them as they stared down into the glistening surface, giving each of them the feeling as if they were actually walking on ice.

The windows were covered with designs from what had to be one of the most talented artists to ever pick up a paint brush who the Clifton's later found out was a local talent from the very city of Nashville himself named Terrance Le'mont London. Which also, in fact, amazed them all. Living in the city of Nashville most of their lives, if not all, the Clifton's had no idea that this type of history even existed. And the recruiters were incredible in their passionate way of explaining it to them.

So, as they delved through fact after fact about one historical figure to another, Big John's focus remained on Henry "Box" Brown, who received his freedom by mailing himself by crate from the slave infested state of Virginia to the free lands of Philadelphia, Pennsylvania, by boxing himself up as cargo. Where he stored more than enough food for the twenty-seven-hour journey with the assistance of James C. A. Smith, a free black man, and Samuel A. Smith, a Caucasian shoemaker who placed a "dry goods" sticker on the outside of the box and also made the arrangements of shipping Henry to the office of Quaker Merchant Passmore Williamson, another reliable and very dependable source of friends.

As Big John described in intricate detail Henry "Box" Brown's amazing escape to freedom,

Potential could hardly believe his ears and hung onto his grandfather's every word in pure astonishment. He wondered how a man that was prohibited from reading and writing could possibly plan something so spectacularly genius and actually get away with it.

As the words of Grandma Clifton instantly entered his mind. "All things are possible with God," Grandma Clifton would religiously quote. As Potential repeated the words underneath his breath while following his grandfather to another famous and very courageous abolitionist by the name of Gabrielle Prosser.

"Prosser, who although was unsuccessful in the leading of his early 1800's slave revolt against the whites of Richmond, Virginia due to the betrayal from another fellow slave exposing his plans, still captured America's undivided attention with this very courageous act in hopes of retrieving his freedom. And is still glorified as a martyr amongst our people until this very day," the recruiter stated as Potential stared at the pictures that hung before him in awe, secretly comparing the features of his ancestors to that of himself.

The wide nose, full lips and the extremely powerful bone structure in their features, Potential possessed as well, along with the very same muscular physique. Which sent a feeling of pride traveling throughout the course of his entire body as he beamed proudly. He held his head up higher, poking out what little of a chest he had at the time even further, and did everything in his power to try and mimic the strengthened posture, of all the heroic figures that currently surrounded him.

Witnessing the reaction of his grandson made Big John proud. He was remembering the time that he himself felt the exact same way upon receiving the enlightenment of who he really was as a black man, and from where and what type of incredible people that he had actually come, finally giving him the ability to sift through the lies that society constantly tried to thrust upon him as an African American male.

And Potential would now have the opportunity to do the same. The confliction between truth and lies tugged at the inner most-deepest parts of Potential's young anatomy, suddenly drifting him into a world of mass confusion as he tried his best to decipher the different emotions without giving into his still very immature understanding. Although he felt joy, happiness, strength and courage, anger still loomed within him as well. And honestly, Potential didn't know why?

Never realizing that it was the spiritual connection that linked him to men such as Henry "Box" Brown, Gabrielle Prosser, Denmark Vessey, Nat Turner and all the many other African American patriots that fought, died, marched, and shed their blood to help bring justice and equality to the black men here in America. But in their attempts of doing so, they were savagely beaten, killed, maimed, and even hanged. Potential's breathing became erratic as he gradually moved through the museum, retaining every word that was being expressed to him by his grandfather and recruiter's alike about the early beginnings of his ancestor's and their cruel and very disturbing experiences here in this country.

And watching the tormenting truth slowly eat away at his grandson's young soul, Big John sat back and allowed Potential to take it all in without saying a word. "This he needs," Big John reasoned amongst himself, keeping a close eye on Potential's very distraught state-of-mind, knowing that he would eventually bring balance to the young man's mental anguish by teaching him exactly how to channel all those negative feelings into something extremely more powerful over time.

He would teach him so he would become victorious over his hatred and not just another statistic of America's vicious and very biased penal system where there were currently over two million people enslaved within the systems walls and more than forty percent of them being black.

It was statistics such as this that Big John feared most. He knew exactly how it felt to be a target. Because he, himself, had been a target since the very first day that he exited his mother's womb in this so-called land of the free as well. But in his opinion, that quote didn't consider black folks at all.

Big John's suffering had been immensely severe growing up in the south. He lived during a time where lynching's, beatings, rapes, and bombings of innocent churches were all normal. And although times had drastically changed for the better, racism hadn't. It had only disguised itself under a new name, "the judicial system," where blacks still received harsher punishments, mainly because of the color of their skin, more so than from actually committing the crime which big John swore that Potential would never be a part of. As he looked up from his grandson's perturbed face and witnessed the beautiful big brown eyes of Emmett Till staring down upon him. "Be sure to protect him, Big John. Make sure that you protect him," Big John heard him whisper.

It was the eyes of Emmett Till that brought the horrible events of his young innocent life instantly flooding back to the full front of his mind. As the images of Emmett's disfigured appearance once again flashed before Big John's eyes, causing him to recoil. All of a sudden it was 1955 all over again and big John was seated in the living room amongst his family reading a magazine when he came across a picture so gruesome it made him drop the book entirely. A picture of Emmett Louis Till's deceased body.

A beautiful, strong young African American male from Chicago, Illinois who tragically lost his life at the tender age of fourteen in the racist city of Money – Mississippi, for allegedly whistling at a white woman.

Although Emmett Till's trial received national and international coverage from the press, and lasted a total of five full days, which might I add was a world record in Mississippi for a black man, at the time, the culprits who were responsible for his murder were found not guilty, and it only took the jury no longer than an hour to decide their fate. Which caused many African American communities all across the country to respond with anger, with Big John and his family being one of them.

Rehashing these brutal events still held the same effect on him now that they did back when he was only a child. A very strong sense of unhealthy, but controllable anger rushed his normally calm demeanor, sending a single tear stubbornly streaming from his eye. He aggressively wiped his face with the palm of his huge, calloused hand as if he was trying to eradicate the thoughts from his mind forever. And with anger in his heart, Big John began to pray.

Grabbing Potential's hand and pulling him down into a kneeling position in the presence of all of their ancestor's and family members alike, he constantly asked his Lord and Savior, Jesus Christ for his profound provision.

And kneeling beside his grandfather, but never closing his eyes, nor bowing his head as the others had done, Potential felt that prayer was purposeless. After all, it had never stopped the atrocious acts of southern whites from taking the lives of all the many innocent men, women and children that hung on the wall before him, had it? And it definitely wouldn't stop them from trying to take his, he sadly thought to himself.

Knowing after today's visit to FCA's amazing African American museum, he would never again be the same.

Finally exiting the museum's doors with Big John's arm flung around his tiny, little shoulders as he slightly shielded his eyes from the brightness of the sun, Potential's resentment grew even stronger as he noticed the two white detectives that was standing at the bottom of the steps making a request for his sister.

"Talent Clifton, we would like to ask you a few questions concerning the kidnapping and aggravated assault of an, uuummm......," the short stubby detective hesitated while looking over the documents that he held clinched between his chubby little fingers. Finding what he was looking for he continued, "an Elizabeth Clifton," he confusingly stated scowling at the papers as if he was actually reading it wrong. But he wasn't. He noticed that they both possessed the same last name and somehow had to be related.

"Elizabeth Clifton!" Grandma Clifton shouted. "Sir, you must be mistaken because Talent and Liz are cousins, and our family ties are tight!" Mrs. B. Lee said with Survivor following suit just as Grandma Clifton fell to her knees, gasping for air from the shock of the news. She was clutching at her chest as if she was having a heart attack, which she quickly realized she was.

"Noooooo!" Potential fearfully screamed, looking into his great grandmother's panic-filled eyes before becoming completely incensed with rage. "This is all your fault! Why don't ya'll just leave us alone!" he aggressively yelled charging the two detectives like a deranged mad man without a weapon, as five loud pops echoed throughout the museum's corridor like fireworks on the 4th of July.

Pop... Pop... Pop... Pop... Pop!

Sending Potential's young body crashing to the pavement in a very awkward position as the entire Clifton family, all except Grandma Clifton, quickly rushed to his side.

"Help me momma, it's hurting me, hurting me badly." Potential weakly whispered before fading into unconsciousness as Survivor hysterically screamed...

"Noooooo!" She yelled pumping furiously on Potential's chest trying her best to revive him... But it was too late, it seemed.

Chapter 1

Potential lays on the ground limp, not moving, and soaked in a thick, red substance that encompasses his entire upper torso.

Survivor frantically pumps Potential's small, deflated chest as her tears continuously fall upon her son's face and neck. Her loved one's hoovered close by, praying that the young life of their relative will be spared yet again, for a third time.

"Please, Lord! Please don't allow my child to be taken away from me like this, Lord! Please!" Survivor hysterically prays, begging God to spare her son.

With tears in her eyes, Survivor stares up at the heavens and pleads to the only one she feels can truly help her at that moment.

Grandma Clifton slowly regains consciousness. She goes to assist Mrs. B. Lee in caring for the broken Survivor as much as they possibly can while trying to attend to Big John.

After brutally attacking the detective who fired the shots at Potential, Big John was restrained in leg and wrist restraints and was being carted away.

The detective wasn't dead, but from the current looks of things, he was probably wishing he was. The whooping that Big John administered to the officer was one of the worst that either family member, or recruiter alike had ever seen.

The grace of Big John's old age became that of a seasoned young man all over again. The actions of the detective pushed him to turn to violence so animalistically cruel as he dipped in and out of being captured while landing one crushing blow after another, until the detective's bruised and battered face was as tender and bloody as that of an uncooked steak.

The detective's partner was traumatized, and with so much fear and confusion inside, he fumbled and dropped his walkie-talkie more than a few times before successfully calling for reinforcement. But he never once thought of pulling his police-issued weapon to assist.

Although Big John's reaction wasn't one that he was proud of, he had little to no regrets about how the situation unfolded. At least, not until he witnessed the weeping eyes of his granddaughter, Talent, who was now being placed in the back of a patrol car and whisked away to the Juvenile Detention Center to face the false allegations that had been conjured up on her by her big cousin, Liz.

Big John had always seen the competitiveness that existed between Talent and Liz over the years, but he always thought of their competition as innocent and somewhat of a good thing. Especially when it seemed to be pushing them both in the direction of becoming better individuals because of it, so he thought.

But for Liz, that was never the case at all. In her mind, Talent's behavior was the ultimate act of betrayal. Acts that would never truly be forgiven by Liz, and losing a fight to her younger cousin Talent, on top of everything else, only seemed to add more insult to Liz's already partially shattered ego.

Talent had always been one to do everything within her power to show Liz up, or to try and make her look bad in front of the rest of their family and friends. Or at least that's what Liz had started to believe. Which, in all actuality, was the furthest thing from the truth. But no one could convince Liz to believe anything other than what she believed to be true, so it was what it was.

At that point, Liz was willing to do whatever it was that she had to do TO WIN!

"By Any Means Necessary!" as the late, great, Malcolm X had once stated in one of his sure-fire speeches during his young life. And Liz surely meant, by any means!

Big John pondered over the actions of his granddaughters for a few minutes more before totally disregarding them for the ones that were currently at hand. He knew that he, and Talent, should both be released sometime soon within the next few hours. Or so he hoped.

Big John sat in the jail cell thinking about the moment he would be released. The first thing he would be doing is getting to the bottom of whatever was brewing between Talent and Liz, once and for all.

Or so he thought, all the while, never fully comprehending the true severity of Liz's jealousy, envy, distastefulness, and resentment towards Talent; the youngest of the two.

Chapter 2

Extremely stiff from his aching muscles as the cold, hard, steel and concrete continuously pressed into his old frame, Big John did everything that he possibly could to make himself comfortable in the cramped confinement of Nashville's extremely filthy, and dilapidated, Criminal Justice Center. A place where men and women from all walks of life were inhumanely held against their will in hopes of someday, once again, becoming free. At least that's what so-called society liked to call it, knowing that most likely they would not be free any time soon due to racial inequality, and so many other systematic roadblocks that presently exist within the American judicial system against black and brown people of this country. Which only added an even stronger sense of disdain and frustration to Big John's distraught train of thought. As he thinks about his situation, he remorsefully shakes his head, following it up with a volatile cringe.

All his life, Big John had either witnessed or experienced, some of the most atrocious and demoralizing acts of mistreatment towards his people firsthand. All were performed by the hands of White Americans, the American Negro's most dangerous threat. With that thought in mind, along with his current predicament, Big John suddenly began to relive the tragic events of Florine Cowan Academy.

The officer, with no hesitation at all, so easily took aim at the innocence of Big John's grandson, firing multiple life-threatening shots. As he reflected on what had happened, it ignited Big John's blood to a boil once again, instantly causing him to bellow out a gut-wrenching scream. Sounds that seemed to have derived from the depths of his soul, and not just from the aching of his aging muscles.

"Aaaarrgghh!" Big John yelped.

Pounding the cold, hard, steel of the holding cell bench, he sat up into an upright position with a look in his eyes that truly expressed his deepest, most inner thought. The other patrons respectfully gave Big John his appropriate space to vent as small particles of DNA dripped from his bruised knuckles.

The other men could relate to Big John's angst. Knowing exactly why he was there only seemed to have bonded the other detanee's to the older man even more. They silently celebrated his victory with him, if you could call it that, connecting them in a way that only the so-called downtrodden and underprivileged black and brown man of America could possibly understand, or relate to.

A pain that only they, the American minority, knew oh so well, and one that could never be denied no matter how hard anyone tried to conceal it, or act as if it did not exist. From a lot of perspectives, especially from most white perspectives, it was solely, "The American Way."

Big John vehemently fumed as he dwelled on his current thoughts. The constant smell of the rancid stench, and the horrendous decor' of his temporary living quarters, only inflamed him even more. An overwhelming feeling of uncontrol and powerlessness rapidly began racking his old, yet very well-cared-for physique in a way that didn't seem humanly possible. This caused Big John to age what appeared to be an additional five to seven years in just that extremely small amount of time.

"Lord, what on earth could possibly be taking these people so long!" Big John frustratingly said as he paced the floor in unbelief. *Be still for I am God!* Big John heard the depths of his inner being soothingly reply. He then hears the confident words of the Prophet Isaiah shortly afterward, *Fear not for I am with you; Be not dismayed, for I am your God. I will strengthen you; Yes I will help you; I will uphold you with my righteous right hand.*

Those who war against you shall be as nothing, as a nonexistent thing. For I the Lord your God will hold your right hand, saying to you, "Fear not, I will help you!"

And upon the completion of that last statement, Big John's name was instantly called.

"John Clifton, is there a John Clifton here?" The mean, ill-spirited, manly-looking correctional officer venomously barked into the extremely cramped confines of the cellblock looking as if she hated to express her next statement.

"John Clifton, you've made bail! Now, grab your junk and get out before I decide to convince the sergeant in charge to purposely alter your paperwork, and lose you in the system for at least another week. You Criminal!" The correctional officer angrily spat as she furiously scrunched her brow into an evil scowl before spitting a huge, discolored loogie onto the pavement right next to Big John's foot where another battered black man lay tightly curled up in a fetal position from some extremely unnecessary, but sickeningly common, police brutality.

Chapter 3

Mad, confused, and very much uncomfortable with her current surroundings, Talent's emotions surfaced like a very intense roller coaster ride, full of extreme twists and turns, along with a barrage of many different ups and downs. She tried to wrap her mind around Liz's repeated acts of betrayal towards her, and the fact that because of them, she was now incarcerated.

For the life of her, Talent could not understand how it had gotten to this point between her and her cousin. Or what she had ever done to Liz to make her so disgruntled and resentful. But obviously it had. And if that was the way that Liz wanted things to be between them, then that's exactly what she would receive in return. Talent was completely fed up with Liz's ugliness.

Talent paced the floor of her cell, to and from the back wall of the small, confined space like a caged animal as she listened to the manic screams and cries of all the other young female hostages that occupied the hellacious living quarters of Nashville's detention center for the youth. Better known to most as "juvie hall."

"Lord, I know that your word says not to repay evil for evil, but to take thought for what is right and honorable. Lord, you also know that I've been constantly trying to stand on your word too, right?" Talent said aloud, bowing her head. She lightly shook it from side to side in total disbelief from the constant slew of emotions that was plaguing her deepest, most inner thoughts in that moment. All Talent could feel in the depths of her soul was an immensely strong and intense sense of revenge that was begging her to be released. Her spirit instantly shifted back to the place where she pleaded, prayed, and fought so incredibly hard to keep it from descending to, on an everyday basis.

A place that was for sure backwards for Talent, back to the horrible and dreadful day when Talent had mercilessly beaten her cousin Liz unconscious for bullying her as a younger child. She also thought back to that unforgettable day, not too long ago, when she had stabbed, fought, and violently defended herself against a fellow schoolmate for constantly mimicking some of those same actions towards her years later. Only to find out that Liz was also responsible for that situation, as well, suddenly shattering Talent's heart into a thousand pieces once again.

Talent had allowed Liz to get away with far too much over the years due to her current belief in God. She thought about how wrong she had been for thinking that sparing Liz from the wrath of her two ex-best friends, Shica and Sheena, would possibly open her eyes to her wrongs, maybe even causing Liz to change her wicked ways. But even that didn't work.

Now it was time for Liz to pay. And pay for her demonic ways she surely would, Talent promised herself. She violently wiped away the tears that were cascading from her doe-like eyes, formulating themselves into a tiny puddle in the center of the floor. Before suddenly adding to the chaos that surrounded her on every side by releasing a few manic screams of her own. The scream was so loud that it seemed to vibrate both concrete and steel.

"Aaaarrgghh!"

Talent frustratingly yelled into the dank, dimly-lit room that contained only a thin plastic-covered piece of material that sufficed as a mattress for the youth detention center's bed. Furiously pounding on it until her fist began to ache. Which only seemed to have infuriated Talent even more.

"I'm gonna get you back for this Liz! I'm definitely gonna get you back for this. I swear!" Talent sacredly vowed.

Grandma Clifton's words appeared in Talent's head once again, wreaking havoc like the violence of a massive tornado; twisting, turning, and disassembling all three major parts of Talent's brain; the cerebrum, the cerebellum, and the brainstem, until all rational thinking on her behalf had completely dissolved.

Once again leaving Talent screaming at the walls of her small cell, or to whomever else was listening at the moment, feeling as if she was on the verge of losing her mind.

"Get me out of here, Lord! Please, get me out of here! I need you!" Talent screamed out as she sobbed. She fell to her knees, clutching herself into a human-size ball before easing back towards the corner of the cold, metal frame of her bunk. Talent incoherently mumbled a few other words into her knees, hoping and praying that her Lord and Savior was listening.

God must have been listening because just as the last words escaped Talent's mouth, the huge, steel door of the cell simultaneously swung open as well.

"Talent Clifton, all of your paperwork has been processed and your family is here to pick you up. You're free to go home young lady!" The pod officer stated. He acknowledged that Talent was one of the few that truly didn't belong inside of that place, as he side-stepped to give her access to the hallway where he would then escort Talent through yet another huge, steel, framed door, where she would exit the facility.

"Thank you, Lord! Lord, thank you!" Talent earnestly expressed walking extremely close to the officer, in hopes that it wasn't a mistake.

Chapter 4

Talent shielded her eyes from the sun, after exiting the detention center doors. She walked to the awaiting car and climbed into the backseat of the vehicle. Big John and Talent both sat immensely quiet. Mrs. B Lee smoothly navigated the big sedan towards the hospital where Potential was occupying the exact same bed that his mother frequented earlier that year after losing her battle to anxiety.

Potential was steadily fighting for his life. From Survivor's perspective, things weren't looking too promising for her child at the moment. She tried desperately to stifle her sobbing by covering her face with the towel that was tightly clenched between her fingers.

All the tape, gauze, tubes, fluids, IVs and loudly beeping monitors that were attached to Potential's small body in some way or another, had Survivor trembling with fear, paralyzing her from head to toe as she refused to be removed from the room. Survivor's body was completely numb. Just as well as her mind. And although she worked in this type of environment almost daily, nothing that she previously encountered, up until that point, could ever prepare her for what she was experiencing as she stared at her son in total disbelief. She closely monitored the horrifying stillness of Potential's riddled frame, which on more than several occasions didn't appear to be moving. The sight of her son gave Survivor that familiar feeling as if she was on the verge of having another serious breakdown.

Nervously gnawing most of her fingernails down to actual knubs, something that Survivor did as a child while in deep thought, she fretfully began worrying about the rest of her family members, wondering why it was taking them so long to make it to the hospital as a tad bit more of Survivor's paranoia rapidly begin presenting itself to the world with each and every passing moment.

Fidgeting was becoming a part of Survivor's norm as she paced the floor, unable to be still. Unconsciously bringing herself to a slight gallop, Survivor's sweat glands suddenly kicked into overdrive, releasing perspiration from places on her body that she never knew existed until that very moment.

"Protect my family, Lord. Please allow them to be okay!" Survivor exasperatedly pleaded.

The circumference within the quaint little hospital room suddenly seemed to be closing in on

Survivor from every direction. Instantly, her breathing increased to that of a world-renowned sprinter who had become completely fatigued, but still gave it all that they had in order to finish the race.

Survivor could hear the chants and cheers of the crowd continuously willing her forward in her head. But the aching of her lungs and the cramping of her muscles would not be denied. Although none of this was actually real, Survivor could still somehow envision herself face down on the pavement, just as she had been many months ago in front of the hospital. Diminishing her breathing even more so now, as a small twinge of light-headedness begins to sneak into the fold.

"I can't handle another tragedy, Lord! I promise I can't!" Survivor stated.

She desperately fell to her knees in total submission, unconsciously scratching places on her body that didn't even itch at the moment. She repeatedly tugged on the collar of her shirt in hopes of creating some type of positive airflow for her overheating body in which was highly unsuccessful.

Survivor's body temperature increased even higher, and the black flashing dots were present just as before. She could feel herself fading fast. No one could hear her screams as she yelled. But then it happened...

The voice.

The same soft spoken and very distinctive voice that she heard before, was back, and confidently assuring her that this too would be alright as well. The voice granted Survivor a state of confidence that somehow appeared unnatural, causing a heaviness to her eyelids that she couldn't manage to control or keep open no matter how hard she tried.

The soothingly soft voice quietly quoted a scripture that Survivor hadn't read more than once or twice in her lifetime, and surely had not memorized, yet, and still, there it was clear as day.

"Come to me, all who labor and are heave laden, and I will give you rest. Take my yoke upon you and learn from me, for I am gentle and lowly in heart, and you will find rest for your souls. For my yoke is easy and my burden is light."

The soothing voice continuously whispered to Survivor over and over again, in the sincerest of tones, instantly relieving her from all of her current anxieties and replacing them with the barely audible purrs of her childlike snores. Survivor comfortably positioned her body in the chair that resided right next to Potential's hospital bed. She was completely oblivious to the constant fluttering of her son's eyelids as they repeatedly tried forcing themselves open.

Chapter 5

Jolted from his slumber and totally oblivious to his current surroundings, Potential took a full observation of the strange environment in which he resided before noticing that he was in the hospital.

Then all of a sudden, just like a hard slap to the face, in order to help jar his dazed memory back to reality, the horrid events of Florine Cowan Academy instantly came flooding back into Potential's mind. Anger consumed him like that of a category five hurricane.

Violent!

Destructive!

And full of fury!

Within seconds Potential was frantically trying to hoist himself from the bed. But nothing seemed to be working at the time, except for the erratically beeping monitors that he was connected to. The beeping sounds awakened Survivor from her much-needed rest but had also alerted Nurse Vickie and several other members of her nursing staff to Potential's room in a hurried fashion.

"Momma! Momma, what's happening to me?" Potential nervously tried screaming through the tubes in his mouth, but only he could fully understand what he was saying. Survivor stared into the panic-filled eyes of her young son, wishing that she could read his mind in that moment. But for the life of her, she could not make out what he was trying to say, no matter how hard she tried.

Potential vigorously snatched and pulled against his restraints like an enraged beast, completely unaware that he was strapped to the bed for his very own safety. Several hours prior, while being admitted into the hospital, he had thrown a fit causing him to be restrained to prevent him from hurting himself and to keep the bullets from traveling any further inside his body, in hopes of possibly preventing any more internal damage to his organs.

Throughout the years in nurse Vickie's line of work, she had witnessed many young African Americans, both male and female, inadvertently meet their fate due to something as simple as the traveling of a bullet. One of which was her very own nephew, Terrance, her big brother Frank's only son. Frank had also been tragically taken down by gun violence as well just a few years prior to that of his child.

Two totally unrelated incidents, on two totally different relatives of hers, but bearing the same impact and fate: Death! Losing them both is something that nurse Vickie would never truly forget or get over for as long as she lived. But also, something that she would definitely use as motivation to continuously propel herself forward in life in order to help as many of her people that she most possibly could. She wanted to do just as the prominent Dr. Dorothy Lavinia Brown, one of her most admired role models had done within her lifetime as well.

Dr. Dorothy Lavinia Brown was one of Tennessee's most inspiring intellectuals, and surely one of the most mentally assertive African American women that has ever resided in the city of Nashville, or who has ever participated in the field of medicine at all, from a lot of people's perspective. A woman who had not only studied, but who also graduated from the world renowned Meharry Medical College in 1948, and did her five-year residency under another prestigious and highly acclaimed negro physician, Chief Surgeon, Dr. Matthew Walker Sr., a man who Dr. Dorothy L. Brown deemed extremely brave by accepting her into his program despite the advice from his staff and their beliefs that a woman couldn't possibly withstand the rigors of surgery.

Not only did Dr. Brown withstand the difficulties of surgery, but she also excelled in it, becoming the very first African American female surgeon in the entire south at the time. Her success was followed by a plethora of several other firsts as well. Like becoming the first African American female representative in the state legislature in Tennessee. In which, she later resigned due to the bitter defeat of an expanded abortion rights bill that she sponsored, and believed had the ability to save a vast number of lives for women within the state.

It was because of this type of passion, commitment, and determination that was embedded into great women such as, Dr. Dorothy L. Brown, that had inspired nurse Vickie into becoming a nurse as well. She had hopes and aspirations of someday becoming and doing even more in life in the near future as she tirelessly trudged through the final months of medical school, aiming towards becoming a doctor herself.

Becoming a doctor is something that nurse Vickie had always envisioned for herself, and she made it top priority, devoting her life to follow in the footsteps of the greats; the Dr. Dorothy L. Brown's, the Dr. Matthew Walker Sr's, and the now highly sought after African American ophthalmologist, Dr. J. C. Wiseman of Meharry Hospital.

Upon the completion of her previous thoughts, nurse Vickie beamed with pride, fully satisfied with her current accomplishments. She instinctively snaps back into nurse mode with the barking of her orders, after witnessing Potential's extremely irate behavior, somewhat startling everyone with the tone of her voice.

"Nurse Ransom, check the straps on both of his feet! Ms. Allison, you check the straps on his left wrist. I got this one!" Nurse Vickie authoritatively commanded. She swiftly took action before rushing to Potential's right side and checking his restraints. She gently placed the palm of her left hand on his forehead and soothingly quoted the very first scripture that came to mind, which happened to be the exact same scripture that Survivor had prayed over her son's life several years before after being given the mysterious drawing that Potential had created for her with the word "Love" somehow etched through the center of its heart.

"Lord, give charge over your angels concerning this young man, to guard him in all of his ways. For in their hands, they shall protect him and bear him up." Nurse Vickie solemnly recited the sacred words of Psalms 91:11 before continuously mumbling onward until finally finishing up whatever else it was that she was asking of God.

Nurse Vickie never once acknowledged the puzzled expression that was plastered upon Survivor's flustered face. As the words of her very own prayer several years prior, along with the very first discussion that she had ever had with the McCreary's, all instantly came flooding back into

Survivor's mind like that of a tsunami! Her mouth hung open in disbelief, while she stared into space.

"Survivor! Survivor, what's wrong? Girl, you don't look too good. Are you okay?" Nurse Vickie asked. She had the most genuine of intentions. Survivor didn't respond so Nurse Vickie gently nudged her shoulder, but she still received no response.

Nurse Vickie wrote it off as nothing more than stress and that Survivor didn't want to speak. She politely turned her undivided attention back to Potential, as he slowly drifted back towards the land of dreams after receiving the sedative administered into his IV in order to help keep him calm. Survivor, with her doe-like eyes fixated on Potential, fretfully watched her child with extreme caution without speaking a word.

Nurse Vickie closely accessed the entire situation from beginning to end making a mental note to bring Survivor something back to help her relax as well.

"Nurse Ransom, page Dr. Gavel for me, and notify him to prepare for an emergency surgery because the fragment that's protruding from this young man's chest cavity has to be removed right now!" Nurse Vickie stated before double-checking each of Potential's restraints for a second time, making sure that they were all properly fastened and secured.

Chapter 6

Everyone from within the Clifton family had finally arrived at the hospital just as Potential was being wheeled into surgery. Their emotions were on edge to the highest degree, and you could tell their nervousness had obviously taken over the place of their once unusually calm and poised demeanor. Calm and poise is something that the entire Clifton clan seemed to have possessed in one way or another as if it was some type of character trait that had been blessedly bestowed upon them all by God himself.

Almost every woman within the family was a complete mess. But none of them seemed to be taking it harder than Talent. She blamed herself for this entire ordeal. She felt that she was the reason Potential had rushed the officers in the first place.

As a sudden influx of tears poured from Talent's eyes, she passionately sent prayers up to God on her little brother's behalf. The stress of the situation had her weak and quivering to the point that you could barely understand anything she was saying. Her state was making the majority of her other family members sad as well.

Talent stumbled away from the family to gather herself, passing Liz along the way, but Talent didn't acknowledge her in the least.

Liz was completely dumbfounded in a sense. She just knew that her little cousin would be seeking revenge towards her for sure after her last embodiment of work. But Liz was puzzled that Talent was not reacting to her being there. She narrowed her eyes into tight, little slits, and stared at Talent from across the room. Liz disliked her cousin even more for once again messing up another one of her so-called plans.

Talent did notice Liz's presence and was also aware of the perplexities within her spirit when she didn't respond the way that Liz had expected her to. That only stemmed even more confusion into Liz's already child-like state of mind before she could possibly recover.

Talent inwardly celebrated the small sense of victory that she currently received from her big cousin's reaction. She grinned and once again pushed her and Liz's differences to the furthest parts of her mind. She would be sure to address and handle the issues later. *But today obviously wasn't the appropriate time nor place*, Talent thought.

Talent refocused her undivided attention back towards Potential. She was still passionately praying that he would pull through yet again. Talent couldn't possibly imagine living life without the annoying behavior of her baby brother.

An aggressively charged series of stomach cramps repetitively began attacking Talent's innermost difficult to reach organs with such an intensity that it brought Talent to her knees. Talent clutched herself into a small, human-size ball just as she did inside of the detention center's holding cell. Talent courageously tried embracing the pain as best as she possibly could while begging God to spare the life of her little brother instead of her very own, if it were to come to that.

As she continuously grimaced in pain, she quoted the verses of Psalms 119 starting with verse 145.

"I cry out to You with my whole heart; hear me, O' Lord! I will keep Your statues. I cry out to You; save me and my brother, and I will keep Your testimonies. I rise before the dawning of the morning, and cry for help. I hope in Your word." Talent coherently professed.

As the images of her brother's body laying sprawled across some operating room table seared themselves within her mind, she continued praying.

"Watch over my little brother, Lord! Please, watch over him for us!" Talent was consumed with visible tears and crying even harder. Talent desperately wished for all her pain to just magically disappear. But she quickly realized that it would not.

Talent's mournful cries were heartbreaking, even to Liz, who for the very first time in a long time, appeared to actually feel something other than hatred or resentment towards her cousin.

That moment for Liz was short lived when she saw all the women in their family, Liz's mother included, quickly rush to Talent's side to console her. Witnessing the display of affection for Talent from them instantly snatched all those mushy, sentimental emotions completely from Liz' thoughts.

Her heart was automatically filled with more rage than ever before towards the little brat that Liz had no choice but to claim as her relative. Liz's face became as hard as granite stone. Liz witnessed the faux act that Talent was currently displaying in order to gain the attention of the family, and it made her sick to her stomach. She thought not only was Talent stealing the attention from her this time around, but from Potential as well. Her very own brother!

Liz psychotically rationalized that Talent didn't care that her brother was possibly dying in some surgery room somewhere deep within the dank, darkened, parts of the hospital. A place where regular civilians and non-surgeons were not allowed. And to Liz, Talent didn't seem to care at all.

Angrily pushing herself out of her seat, Liz undetectably made her way out of the waiting room area. She rudely brushed past the McCreary's without saying a word, vowing to herself to finally get rid of Talent Clifton once and for all...BY ANY MEANS NECESSARY!

Chapter 7

Several grueling hours passed, and Dr. Gavel was finally making his way to the hospital's waiting quarters to deliver the details of Potential's surgery. Everyone present seemed to be holding their breath, hoping, praying, and nervously awaiting what they all wanted to believe to be a positive outcome. But from the hesitation in Dr. Gavel's stride, and the current slump of his shoulders, the Clifton's, suddenly didn't seem to be feeling so well.

Survivor lost full control of her knees. Big John rapidly responded, catching his daughter's collapsing body just seconds before the temple of her head viciously slammed into the acute edge of the hospital's waiting room table, preventing the family from dealing with yet another devastating catastrophe.

Piercing screams echoed from the lungs of all awaiting women, including Mrs. Ida B. and Dorothy, who were just as much affected by the almost horrific turn of events more so than anyone. To the McCreary's, they were all family at this point and pigmentation of skin tones didn't, nor would it, ever determine that factor for any of them. The McCreary's openly made that fact known, and loyally stood shoulder to shoulder with the Clifton's on whatever platform that presented itself. It didn't matter how dangerous that platform appeared to be. They fully understood that the Clifton's were extremely loving and God-fearing people. A very tough group of loving people, but God-fearing all the same.

This was no different than what the famous Caucasian abolitionist John Brown and his son's did, standing juxtaposed with heroic men such as Shields Green, Dangerfield Newby, John Copeland, Lewis Leary, and Mr. Osborne Anderson, in battle until death. The shedding of blood furthermore solidified the strength of their bond all in hopes of ridding the South of its unbearably cruel, inhumane, and extremely atrocious acts of savagery towards African Americans called "slavery" by launching the attack on Harper's Ferry - which, in turn, also ignited the Civil War shortly afterwards.

The McCreary's vowed to stand side by side with the Clifton's just the same, welcoming death as well if it came to that.

T. Thomas instinctively found himself within arm's reach of Grandma Clifton, Mrs. B. Lee, and Talent, just in case either of them needed his assistance after the reading of Dr. Gavel's results. Although, he was truthfully grateful after the fact that neither of them did.

Dr. Gavel flowed through the process with ease. Completely relieving every family member from their worries. He fully explained certain words, breaking them down into much simpler forms for some due to his complex medical terminology that he often used while speaking. He giggled at the faces of certain family members and friends, with Big John being the main culprit. Dr. Gavel respectfully apologized before proceeding forward.

"Sorry for all the medical jargon you guys. I was wondering why you were looking at me as if I had three eyes, or a huge booger hanging from my nose or something." Dr. Gavel humorously stated before he realized the inappropriateness of his latter remark. But Big John and a few other relatives comforted him with their laughter. Instantly placing Dr. Gavel back at ease.

"Did he say booger?" Big John surprisingly questioned releasing another chuckle of his own, before continuing. "Booger huh? Dang Doc, I never would've expected a word like that to come outta your mouth. Me, personally, I would've expected you to call it some type of mucous inclined compounding fixture of slimy decent, or something. But never just a plain ole' ordinary booger!" Big John laughed once again. He finalized the last of his statement with, "Man, you're alright with me!" He threw up the Black Power fist afterwards.

Dr. Gavel confidently reciprocated the gesture with a tad bit more emphasis than had been expected, ending it with a, "Right On!" He left everyone in stitches, laughing for the very first time since Potential's incident.

They conversed with Dr. Gavel about a few other things outside of surgery and medicine. He assured them that everything was going to be perfectly fine, and that Potential's recovery time would solely be up to him and how well he responded to the traumatic effects of being shot. Dr. Gavel let the Clifton's know that it could possibly be weeks, months, maybe even years before Potential fully recovered.

In either case, everyone was still extremely elated, fully understanding, and very much appreciative of the fact that God had once again brought their loved one through the valley of the shadow of death. Even if it was with a multitude of several different scars. Scars that Potential would someday hopefully use to show others just how real God is.

The family bowed their heads in prayer together. They were so relieved from the good news that they didn't even realize they were being watched, not only by one individual this time around, but surprisingly by two.

Liz cautiously waved her goodbye to the extremely pleasant occupant of the gray mercury sedan as they slowly eased themselves away from the curb before finally slithering her way back inside of the hospital's waiting room area. Only this time, it was not undetected.

Chapter 8

Realizing that her daughter was no longer amongst the rest of the family, Dricka went in search for her next to oldest child to make sure that she was alright. Plus, she badly needed to take a cigarette break to help calm her nerves because the atmosphere around her was definitely tense, and Dricka knew exactly why.

Even though Dricka is Liz's mother, she also thought that the things Liz had constantly done to Talent over the years were not only unimaginable, but that they were also pretty much unforgivable as well, Dricka thought, and she was actually Dricka's mother. So, Dricka could only imagine just how bitter Survivor and Talent must've been with her child at the moment. Not to mention the rest of the family. But, in either case, Liz was her child, and Dricka would have her back to the end. Even if it meant going up against certain relatives once again, which would definitely be placing them both in a very precarious type of situation. But how could she possibly avoid it.

Pondering over the possibilities and what this situation could actually lead to, was a little disheartening for Dricka. She fully understood the supreme viciousness of the four lionesses that she and her daughter would be facing if it actually were to come to that, honestly admitting to herself that Talent was possibly the most dangerous of them all due to the utilization of her mind.

Her niece was young, Dricka thought. But she was smart, extremely smart, and she knew that was a dangerous combination.

As dangerous as the bite of an Inland Taipan Snake, who, with one bite, releases enough venom to kill one hundred adults, making it the most venomous animal in the world to humans.

And to Dricka, that's exactly what Talent had the potential of becoming if and when provoked. Just as venomous as an Inland Taipan Snake!

Dricka stood silently in the hospital's vestibule, pondering over her current thoughts for a second more while taking long drags from her Kool filter king cigarette. She held the smoke within her lungs longer than usual in hopes of blaming her current dizziness on that instead of what was really plaguing her brain; Talent.

No matter how long Dricka inhaled and kept the smoke captive, nothing seemed to take the place of the images that were now haphazardly displaying themselves within her mind, like that of a cinematic film. And this to Dricka, became a bit more intimidating. Even for her, she honestly admitted. Dricka was a part of the Clifton clan herself, maybe that's really why she felt the way she did.

She exhaled the extremely toxic and foul-smelling contaminant back into the atmosphere in professionally shaped circles, which would eventually dissolve into mid-air over time. But, not before tampering with the innocent nostrils of the non-smokers that passed to and fro. And, definitely not before witnessing Liz calculatingly making her way back towards the hospital, after waving to the driver in a gray sedan.

Sneakily concealing some type of chrome-looking, metal object into the waistband of her shorts. Dricka realized, yet again, that her daughter was up to no good!

Chapter 9

Beep… Beep…Beep…Beep…Beep…Beep…

The EKG monitor echoed throughout the silent room suddenly giving it a creepy feel of being trapped inside of a mausoleum. Potential's stiffened body lay completely motionless, showing little to no signs of life remaining within him except for the sporadic rise and fall of his increasingly enlarged upper torso area. His chest looked to be packed with gauze making it appear three times its normal size.

The swollen, red, eyes of Survivor attentively peered down upon her youngest and only male child to make sure that he was alright. Survivor wanted Potential to move. She needed to know that her son felt her presence there within the room with him. She needed to know that he, himself, was still fighting to live as well. It had been several hours since Dr. Gavel had completed Potential's surgery, he still hadn't moved a smidgen.

Survivor was crushed inside with each tapered breath that her child struggled to take. "Is he breathing! I can't tell if he's breathing! Are these machines affecting my son's breathing! Lord, what's happening!" Survivor painstakingly questioned.

She was on the verge of clearly losing all control, until the comforting hands of Grandma Clifton found their place on Survivor's shoulders, temporarily relinquishing her of all her angst in that moment.

"It's okay baby, Grandma Clifton got you. Relax. Potential is going to be alright," she softly spoke into Survivor's ear. "God has already placed His hedge around that boy of yours, so be still and just let Him work."

Grandma Clifton guided Survivor away from Potential's bedside. They took a seat nearby and Grandma Clifton continued massaging her granddaughter's shoulders, taking Survivor back to the days when she and her siblings were young, making homemade biscuits and ice cream with their grandmother on the weekend. Those days were priceless for Survivor. Irreplaceable even. And she was sure that each of her family members felt the exact same way about those moments because Grandma Clifton always had a way of making everything better.

Even in situations such as this moment, Survivor thought them to be priceless. She slowly drifted in and out of consciousness as the hardworking, calloused-filled hands of Grandma Clifton continued to softly caress her shoulders, neck, and temple areas until she was completely oblivious to her current surroundings. The words of Grandma Clifton consistently ingrained themselves deeply within Survivor's subconscious with assurance. If Survivor didn't know anything else in life, she knew that her grandmother would never tell her anything wrong.

This moment was the first time in Lord knows how long, that Survivor was truly able to finally relax.

Be still baby girl and allow God to do His work. Potential is going to be alright! Survivor reiterated Grandma Clifton's words in her head. Because her grandmother said it, Survivor knew her words to be true. Fully succumbing to her ignored and very sleep deprived body, her child-like snores seemed to intensify greatly with every inhaling gasp. "R-r-r-r-ronc!... r-r-r-r-ronc! R-R-R-R-RONC!"

Chapter 10

Grandma Clifton removed herself from the hospital's recliner and extended it outward in order for Survivor to stretch her legs. She knew her granddaughter hadn't slept since the incident occurred with Potential. And she knew that lack of sleep wasn't a good thing for Survivor.

She fully understood the importance of sleep; that when the body was denied or deprived of such vital things as rest, nutrients, or its appropriate portion of water consumption, how it could possibly shut down on an individual. Eventually causing even more internal and external damages than one could possibly imagine over time, and the family definitely didn't need to be dealing with another crisis.

Nor did Survivor, Grandma Clifton thought to herself. She slightly pecked Survivor's cheek with a small kiss and covered her body with a blanket to help divert the cold, brisk, breeze from the hospital's air conditioning system.

Survivor snuggled into the blanket as if she was a child again. She remembered all the many times that she and the rest of her relatives would solely take full control of Grandma Clifton's entire bed. Survivor found out later from her grandmother that those were moments that Grandma Clifton used to love, but fussed amongst them at times as if she did not.

Mrs. B. Lee watched as her mother cared for her child and could do nothing but smile. She remembered certain times from her own childhood when she continuously basked in the fact that she was blessed with such a loving and caring mother. But she also knew she had an extremely vicious one too. Mrs. B. Lee silently chuckled to herself. She wondered how a woman that was so kind and sweet could possibly be responsible for causing or creating so much mayhem for so many different individuals throughout the earlier parts of her life.

Like almost shooting and killing the father of her very own child, and her husband's mistress at a neighborhood corner store. That's just one incident of many others that Mrs. B. Lee could possibly name. But she decided against it in order to protect the so-called *innocent*, as she sometimes loved to say.

Mrs. B Lee also placed a kiss upon Survivor's forehead. Survivor appeared to be sleeping so peacefully for the first time in a very long while. Which she actually was due to the dream she was currently having pertaining to Potential's two childhood best friends: Cornell and Kendrick.

Cornell and Kendrick were Survivor's good friend Gayle's two oldest kids. A woman that was more like a sister to Survivor instead of a friend due to the bond that they shared. This bond made Cornell, Kendrick and Potential, more like family.

The three boys did everything together, it seemed, spending almost every waking hour together amongst each other either laughing, playing football, wrestling, turning flips, fighting or practicing Bruce Lee karate moves on one another, which always eventually led to someone crying at times and having to be convinced not to go tell on whoever was responsible in order to avoid getting into trouble and possibly being stuck in the house for the remainder of the day. Which none of them ever really wanted; they all would agree before resuming back to whatever they were initially playing, sometimes switching things up altogether just to completely change the entire course of action.

Cornell was the oldest of the three, making him somewhat of the leader in a sense. Almost everything that he did or attempted to do, normally Potential and Kendrick followed suit. Survivor vividly remembered while dreaming and physically smiled in her sleep.

The other members of the Clifton family noticed Survivor smiling and wondered what she was dreaming about. They agreed that it most definitely had to be pleasurable as they all smiled amongst themselves now as well as they continuously observed Survivor and Potential both with a watchful eye.

Survivor enjoyed watching the boys play amongst themselves so freely. Each of them took turns leading their very own games in order to help balance out the small bouts of bickering that would sometimes ensue otherwise if they did not. They needed no parental guidance of any kind to figure out who would lead amongst themselves. They were each very considerate of one another when it came to almost anything that they had ever done together as a group. Solely because they were a team.

Cornell and Potential loved more of the physical games like wrestling, karate, football, flipping, and boxing. Kendrick, on the other hand, loved playing games like Cowboys and Indians, which is exactly what they were playing when Survivor suddenly began hearing Gayle's voice yelling for her children to say their goodbyes to Potential and the rest of their neighborhood friends when it was time for them to come home.

Sadness covered the boy's face like a mask, not just Cornell and Kendrick, but Potential's as well. Survivor cringed in her sleep when she noticed it, becoming a little bit saddened herself now as she whimpered.

Cornell and Kendrick blatantly ignored the first few calls from their mother of course. No one wanted to be stuck in the house in those days. Especially, when a few of your friends were still outside playing, because a glimpse of the sun was still presently showing itself.

Now, the latter of Gayle's calls to her children could not be denied. Cornell and Kendrick both acknowledged her calls when the added aggression and the tad bit more assertiveness existed within her vocals. It was at that time they would finally gather up their belongings to leave, still pushing, shoving, and tugging on a few of their closest childhood friends once or twice more, before looking in both directions then quickly crossing the street.

As they made it to the other side of the street, Cornell and Kendrick slowly turned to say their final goodbye for the night. But it was something about their smile this time that Survivor remembered.

This moment is exactly where Survivor's dream began to take a turn. Cornell and Kendrick were standing in the spot where their home normally resided, but in its place were some very expensive looking pearl-like gates. Gates so massive that they reached the clouds. The streets were no longer concrete. They were gold and reflecting so brightly that Survivor was actually covering her eyes. Even in her sleep.

Gayle continuously called out to Cornell and Kendrick, who by now, were fading deeper and deeper into the thickest, most beautiful, aggregate of white clouds. The clouds were aligned by a lighting so radiant that it made the most crepuscular of rays appear to be dull.

Survivor started stirring in her sleep even more so from the current events of her dream. But still sleeping like a newborn child as Grandma

Clifton repeatedly stroked her granddaughter's hair.

Even though Survivor was dreaming, everything that she was seeing felt so real. Especially, when both boys, Cornell and Kendrick, stated that their childhood best friend was going to be perfectly fine. Hearing them speak those words abruptly awakened Survivor from her peaceful slumber. She wildly looked all throughout the room, until her eyes landed on Potential.

Potential was groggily staring back in his mother's direction. With a raspy voice, a voice that was obviously still extremely weak, but full of determination, he told Survivor about a dream that he had just had about his two childhood best friends that had passed away far too soon.

Survivor's eyes almost popped from their sockets in total disbelief realizing that he too had also been dreaming about Cornell and Kendrick as well.

Chapter 11

Several weeks had passed since Potential's surgery, and his recovery was going better than expected. Dr. Gavel was even surprised with the young man's recovery as well. What he saw he would have deemed impossible had he not been witnessing Potential's healing process for himself first-hand.

The gunshot wound that resided just above Potential's heart was no longer detectable to the naked eye. But the hideous scar that resided in the center of his chest definitely was. Every time Potential saw the scar it caused a very intense anger to well up inside him.

Potential listened to the prayers that were sent up on his behalf from each of his family members. Especially those from Talent, his only sibling whom he loved dearly. Even with the prayers, nothing seemed to diminish Potential's current feelings about certain things that happened to him, and that concerned his family.

Potential wasn't mad or upset with God about anything; he loved God. He loved Him even more so now than ever before. If it had not been for God, Potential knew that he would no longer be dwelling amongst the land of the living. And for that, he was truly grateful.

But it still didn't help absolve the current ugliness that was permanently lodged deeply within Potential's psyche towards the officer who had previously fired the shots. In his heart, just below where he'd been fatally struck just a short time ago, Potential knew that the officer had intentionally tried to annihilate him without giving it a second thought. Because of that, Potential didn't feel that he could ever forgive, no matter how much he believed in God.

The menacing scowl that was plastered across Potential's face appeared to grow harder with each passing thought. Especially, since today would be the first time Potential would be crossing paths with that exact same officer in court.

Potential's health and strength was nowhere near a hundred percent. His energy seemed to evaporate from his body quicker and quicker with each step he took. But the prosecutor didn't hesitate to drag Potential's weak and fragile frame into the courthouse.

His court appearance wasn't to convict or bring charges against the officer who had shot Potential. No, that wasn't the case at all. Potential, Survivor, and the rest of their family had just recently become aware of why they were there. Big John's attorney gave them all a brief summary on what to expect before entering the courtroom.

Afterwards, the attorney notified them that everything was under control. The attorney was privy to the prosecution's tactics in presenting their case. He also had some very vital information that was dropped into his lap by an extremely reliable colleague of his. The colleague heard somewhat of a heated exchange between the two involved officers without the acknowledgement of his presence. He hurriedly passed the information along to his friend which just so happened to be Big John and Talent's defense attorney; the two main individuals that the prosecutor was trying to hold responsible for the entire FCA debacle.

Attorney Arthur Lee, of Arthur Lee Esquire Inc., was an absolute nightmare to the commonalities of Nashville's Judicial System. A system, who for the longest time, had absolutely served no person of color any type of reputable justice of any kind. Even to this very day, honestly speaking, his representation is questionable.

Attorney Arthur Lee was tall, strong, with a mocha-latte brown complexion and distinctly intelligent. He had the athletic build of the highly esteemed and very acclaimed African American boxing legend, Mr. Sugar Ray Robinson. Sugar Ray was a man who is often regarded as the greatest boxer of all time, pound for pound. Even above another one of our absolute greats, Mr. Muhammad Ali.

And just like these two great men of valor, attorney Arthur Lee was built and equipped for battle just the same. He guided the Clifton's to their awaiting seats, while taking a seat of his own next to Big John, who sat immensely poised. They both patiently awaiting the bailiff to finally call their case.

Walking into the courtroom and observing all of the white faces that occupied its space, Potential's mind instantly started reeling back to the auctioneer blocks of slavery. A place that he had now become so knowledgeable of, whether it being through Big John, E. L. Morrow, the FCA recruiter, or from his own reconnaissance by devouring so many different African American history books during his recovery. He watched as one black person after another, both male and female, appeared before the presiding judge, sometimes for the smallest of infractions. Even though small, they were still sentenced to some form of jail time and ushered away in chains.

Potential shook his head in disgust trying to ward off the negativity that was currently plaguing him at the moment. But it seemed to be too late. Although he was young, Potential fully understood, and had learned what had definitely been designed or should I say, preordained in order to hinder his people. Especially the males of his race, he thought. And it appeared that the plight had only managed to thicken over time.

Potential acknowledged the strong resemblance that he shared with each of the individuals that entered the courtroom that day. He compared himself to them just as he had done to the martyrs that hung from the walls of FCA's highly modernized art museum. This caused him to become a little saddened this time around, instead of overjoyed. Mostly due to the blatant discrimination and inequality that his people were receiving within the bile's of most American courtrooms all throughout the country.

He meticulously observed each and every public pretender, not defender, factually sell out each of their so-called clients to the prosecutor with a genuine smile etched across their faces. Not even attempting to help or even trying to negotiate a more feasible deal for them in the least. This sent a cold, shivering, chill down Potential's spine, as he watched most of the court officials laugh, joke, and shake hands as if they'd just completed a huge business transaction on the beautiful greens of some immaculate golf course.

The majority of his people left with their heads cast low, with nothing but gloom written upon their saddened faces, and restraints attached to their darkened skin so tightly that not only did it prohibit them from walking properly, but also showing the discoloration of their palms due to the lack of blood flow or proper circulation.

Potential witnessed not one solitary soul amongst them that seemed to care at all, which once again sent his mind traveling back through time to the many different pictures in his history books. From the pictures alone he had visually witnessed similar features from some of those same exact faces smiling, laughing, and celebrating the gruesome deaths of his ancestors, as they hung and swung from trees. Mostly burned, charred, and sometimes even maimed or decapitated as if it was some type of game. For a lot of Caucasians back in those days, it actually was a game, Potential disheartenedly thought.

His eyes had become clouded with tears of pain. But he refused to allow any tears to fall. He stoically eyeballed the officer who was now placing his left hand on the Bible while raising his right hand to swear to tell the truth, the whole truth, and nothing but the truth.

"So Help You God!" Potential heard the bailiff recite so systematically, as he patiently awaited the officer's response.

Taking a small, pregnant pause, along with some very much needed deep breaths, Officer Long finally stated, "I Do!" with jaws tightly clasped the entire time.

Chapter 12

Finally taking his seat on the witness stand after being sworn in, the officer instantly noticed all of the angry glares that he was receiving from each and every member of the Clifton family. But none of them could attempt to compete with the cold, calculated stare of Potential. If looks could somehow actually extinguish a thing in its entirety, then, Officer Long definitely knew exactly what his fate would've been in that moment.

He slowly turned his undivided attention towards the prosecution table, who at the time, seemed to be putting the finishing touches on whatever line of questioning they had prepared in order to present the strongest possible argument within their case.

The presiding Judge, the honorable J. A. Franklin, carefully viewed the prosecution's team with an act of sternness. Seriously eyeballing the prosecution's lead attorney, Mr. C. J. Franklin, who was of no known relation to one another. If you chose to believe both men's story about it. In a manner that seemed almost threatening, had not Attorney C. J. Franklin suddenly arranged the last of his papers and finally made his way from behind the table and towards the witness stand where Officer Long patiently awaited him.

Prosecuting Attorney, C. J. Franklin, started his questions off in the most subtle of ways. Erectly standing without the slightest of bends from any part of his physique as he simply eased Officer Long into his line of questioning, painting the guy as if he was some type of saint.

He asked him questions about the length of his career, his family life, and the current volunteer work that he had just recently become a part of within the last few months. Which mostly dealt with black, underprivileged kids from highly impoverished neighborhoods. Better known as the ghetto.

Prosecuting Attorney C. J. Franklin's entire mission was to try and paint Officer Long as pure as the word "White," in any of your common Americanized dictionaries, while constantly describing Big John as the mere image of how those same exact dictionaries defined the word "Black."

Black - of a person's state of mind; full of gloom or misery; very depressed. Full of anger or hatred; very evil or wicked. Representing evil, darkness, night, and despair; being the symbol of the eternal struggle between day and night, good and evil, and right and wrong...etc.

This is exactly the message that prosecuting attorney C. J. Franklin wanted to portray. Especially since almost all that were currently present within the courtroom that day were Caucasian. Better known as "white."

A few objections were made by Attorney Arthur Lee on Big John's behalf, but not many, which, the majority of the Clifton's could not understand. Especially since most of them felt that the prosecutor was doing an incredible job at blatantly assassinating their loved one's character while all Attorney Arthur Lee had seemed to do was nod his head a little from time to time.

He attentively listened and scribbled lord knows what on that manilla writing pad of his. That is, until the cross-examination began. That's when the fireworks started! The entire Clifton family agreed.

Even Liz, who sat a few rows back from the rest of the family wearing a smug look upon her face that was so apparently visible that even one with the worst of cataract conditions could still envision, most of the family acknowledged.

The moment that the prosecution rested their argument, they felt more than magnificent about the performance that was just displayed.

Judge J. A. Franklin, then gave the floor over to the defense in order to cross-examine if they decided to do so in which Attorney Arthur Lee most definitely did. He was ready unlike the prosecution team, who seemed to take forever with the preparations of their case. Attorney Arthur Lee, of Arthur Lee Esquire Inc., wasted no time at all. And it was at that point when the Clifton's had finally learned exactly what it was that he had been scribbling in that manilla writing pad of his firsthand.

Attorney Arthur Lee was a beast! A man of men! And a man after God's own heart. Just as King David of the Bible had been described. But the only murder that was committed on his behalf was to the many individuals that had once appeared before him on the witness stand. Individuals who stories he casually assassinated bit by bit, along with most of their character, as well. And Officer Long wasn't to be treated any different.

Attorney Arthur Lee strategically emasculated Officer Long more and more with each probing question. He clearly proved that not only he, but also everything that the prosecution had so diligently tried to build Officer Long up to be, was absolutely faux.

His defense sent Prosecuting Attorney C. J. Franklin into somewhat of a fitful rage, as he bolted from his seat toppling it backwards completely, while screaming at the top of his lungs.

"Objection! Objection! He is badgering the witness your Honor! That is mere hearsay! That's hearsay your Honor! Misappropriation of Facts!" Prosecuting Attorney C. J. Franklin continued to proclaim as he yelled out any and everything that entered his mind at the time in order to deflect some of Attorney Arthur Lee's questioning. He could see the seams of his case slowly being ripped apart.

Judge J. A. Franklin banged his gavel in quick successions trying to, once again, regain sole control of his courtroom. But it appeared to be too late as the bailiffs headed in the direction of the prosecution's table in hopes that this would help calm him down. For the moment it had. But just as soon as Attorney Arthur Lee resumed his damaging onslaught of questioning to Officer Long for a second time, the Prosecuting Attorney C. J. Franklin, exploded once again taking things to completely new heights this time around.

His actions instantly gotten him and every other active member of his team, along with defense attorney Arthur Lee, all dragged into the judge's chambers for some sort of deliberation. That didn't appear to be going so well either.

The yelling could be heard throughout the courtroom, as the bailiffs were again summoned to help restore some type of civility after several contempt of court threats had been made.

Officer Long, still on the witness stand, looked somewhat dumbfounded, but felt even worse than that when he realized he'd somehow possibly blown the case.

The deliberation went on a little longer than twenty minutes between the two sides, but the yelling had subsided tremendously. Mostly because of the presence of the big, burly bailiffs, I'm sure. Once all of the smoke had finally cleared, and the courtroom was once again back in its rightful standings, Judge J. A. Franklin eventually dismissed all charges against Big John which overtime would also lead to the dismissal of

Talent's case as well. Especially, after the serious discussion that the entire Clifton family recently had with Liz on Talent's behalf days prior. Which, didn't sit well with Liz at all.

But, for now, Liz would have to agree in order to carry out the latter part of her plan towards her cousin. Spitefully, eyeballing Talent from a distance, Liz walked out of the courtroom solemnly making a promise to herself to eventually repay Talent for all of the embarrassment that she caused her over the years.

Looking up, Liz took notice of the exact same individual that she had once seen outside of the hospital in the white lab coat. She deemed it kind of odd for them being there at first, but suddenly disregarded it due to the fact that they were a doctor.

Liz and Dricka kept strolling, praying that they could hurriedly make it to her mother's car, so that Liz would no longer have to be in the presence of their family. Especially Talent! Liz hatefully grimaced, distastefully spitting on the ground in pure disgust, just before entering the vehicle. Constantly nodding her head back and forth with every disturbing thought.

Chapter 13

Talent was ecstatic with the outcome of her grandfather's court decision and knew that it was only a matter of time before the bogus charges that Liz had brought against her would eventually be annulled as well. But that still didn't diminish the fact that Talent wanted revenge! And this time she would get it! Talent thought. Not only for herself, but for each and every individual that Liz had ever crossed in her entirely miserable little life. The patrons on that list were many.

The cheers were deafening after the rendering of Judge J. A. Franklin's verdict. And although, it was an extremely exciting moment for them all at the time, Talent was still able to somehow capture the evil glares that Liz had shot her way just before exiting the courtroom.

Only this time, they were reciprocated tenfold!

Talent acknowledged the hatred within her cousin's eyes and witnessed that it had grown tremendously over the past few months. But this time she wouldn't attempt to worry about it.

Liz despised Talent for her own personal reasons. To Talent, that much was obvious, and she was done trying to figure out why. She fully came to grips that she never would. Talent had leaned on God about this situation on more than a dozen different occasions, only to somehow be given the same exact answers every time.

Several different instances existed all throughout the course of the Bible where certain relatives or siblings had conducted themselves in some of these exact same ways. So Talent was fully aware of just how serious she and Liz's current circumstance could possibly become. Sibling and relative rivalries dated as far back as the beginning of time, starting with Cain and Abel just to name a few. Talent thought.

Then, there was Ishmael and Isaac. Esau and Jacob. Leah and Rachel. Just in case you only thought that it happened amongst men. Joseph and his brothers, apart from Benjamin, who was not born at the time of Joseph's betrayal. Along with Abimelech and his brother's as well.

In either case, each of these rivalries all led to one or many relatives taking extremely foolhardy, sinful, and most of the time, severely dangerous or detrimental actions towards one another. The exact same actions that Liz had continuously perpetuated towards Talent on more than many different occasions during the short existence of their lives. And now it was time for Talent to gladly return the favor, she thought.

She nodded her head in full agreement with her inner thoughts, while contemplating on reaching out to Shica and Sheena, Liz's two ex-best friends, who actually couldn't stand how Liz had been trying to treat Talent behind her back. She quoted a famous saying that she heard somewhere before, but, truly unable to remember from where. It went something like, "An enemy of my enemy, is definitely a friend of mine!" Talent confidently recited.

Slowly pushing herself to freedom from the confines of the courthouse doors, she allowed the heated rays of the brightly illuminated sun to softly peck her smooth caramel complected skin while singing along to one of James Brown's most popular tunes, "The Payback," as it blared from the speakers of a passing automobile, just as Talent was climbing into the backseat of her grandfather's big sedan. She then heard the exact same song playing on Big John's radio as well when he cranked up the volume and smoothly eased out into traffic.

Big John said to himself, "The radio station couldn't possibly be playing a better song at this moment."

And little did he know, Talent absolutely agreed.

Chapter 14

Storming into her room once arriving home, Liz dove onto her bed burying her face within the pillow in order to muffle the screams that could no longer stay within her body. She yelled at the top of her lungs. She didn't really care who heard her at the moment because that's just how irritated she had become from the thoughts of actually dropping the charges on Talent. Her Nemesis! Her Adversary! Her Archenemy!

But this is what the family requested of her. So, in a sense, she had no choice. Or did she, Liz thought.

"How could they ask me to do this! What if I don't? Will they somehow treat me even worse than they already do! Impossible! It can't get any worse than this!" Liz angrily spat answering all of her very own questions in somewhat of a delusional manner.

She yelled into her pillow once again. This time, adding a vicious bite and wishing that it was some part of Talent's body. She tried her best to release some of the tension that had obviously been stored up inside of her for the past several years. But no matter how loud she screamed, or how hard she yelled, nothing seemed to dissipate Liz's current feelings.

What she was feeling could definitely be identified as pure, unadulterated, revulsion towards her cousin. And, like I said before, she no longer cared who knew it.

Liz taunted the air, while aggressively addressing the furniture of her bedroom as if Talent was actually present. Disliking her cousin more and more with every word she spoke as she continued to openly yell at the walls.

Liz grabbed the abnormally large stuffed animal with Talent's picture taped to its head and repeatedly punched it until she had become fatigued. She was wishing that it was her cousin for real. But even though it was not, just the thought of actually punching something with Talent's face attached to it definitely made Liz feel better. The perspiration that now appeared upon her forehead, slowly began cascading downward causing Liz's entire face to glisten.

A devious grin suddenly appeared upon Liz's face instantly turning her extremely attractive appearance to one that had become immensely darkened, just by the hint of her smile. Her expression revealed every thought or idea that must've been playing within her disturbed little mind at the moment. She smiled even broader at herself in the mirror truly loving the individual that was staring back at her to the fullest.

This person was beautiful, Liz thought. Intelligent, attractive, strong, deceptive, crafty, and sweet. Everything that she had once used to manipulate almost every other person that had ever entered her life in one way or another. Everyone except for Talent.

In the basement of Sheena's home, they had all made a fool out of her, Liz rationalized. And eventually all of them were going to pay for that, she proclaimed. But none of them was held more responsible for her humiliation than Talent.

She pounded the stuffed animal with Talent's face attached to it once again in a blind rage, before ripping its head off completely but still clawing at its eyes until the picture was destroyed. She never once looked up to acknowledge if anyone else was present.

Her mother Dricka looked on in absolute bewilderment, completely horrified by her daughter's actions, especially once she recognized the face that had adorned the decapitated stuffed animal.

"Liz! What On Earth Are You Doing!" Dricka surprisingly yelled leaving her daughter stumped for words for the first time in her life.

Liz racked her brain for a lie but was unable to come up with anything. "Nuh… nuh… nothing momma," Liz sadly stammered back. She looked down at her feet in order to avoid the piercing gaze of her mother's eyes. She felt embarrassed more so for being caught by her mother, instead of for her actions.

Dricka disappointedly stared at her daughter for a moment or two longer before silently exiting the room. She realized that things between her and Talent had gotten completely out of hand, and that there was honestly no turning back for either of them from that point forward.

Dricka silently prayed to her heavenly Father in hopes that He was currently listening. At that moment, Dricka felt that only God could be the one to intervene.

Chapter 15

The images of what Liz had just displayed to her mother had Dricka completely baffled to say the least. So much so, that she instantly prayed for her child, amongst several other things in order for her to better deal with the entire situation as a whole.

She made one last and final request for God to please have patience and mercy on her child, because she definitely knew that Liz was going to need it. Especially if she planned on continuing the pursuit of the likes of her younger cousin Talent. Dricka definitely knew that she would. She was instantly reminded of the times when she and Survivor had traveled down some of those same exact roads back in the days themselves.

The rivalry that existed between Dricka and Survivor was so similar that it almost appeared as if history was once again repeating itself. Or should I say, the rivalry that Dricka had created within herself towards Survivor for her own personal reasons just as Liz was now doing towards Talent.

I guess it was a true statement when the elders of the Clifton family use to repeatedly say, "The apple doesn't fall too far from the tree." In Liz or Dricka's case, it definitely did not. On several different occasions, whether current or previous, this now appeared to be the absolute truth.

Although many, many, years had now passed since Dricka and Survivor's last incident, or encounter with one another, certain thoughts from Dricka's perspective still opened up old wounds. And because of that, Dricka acknowledged that she had never really forgiven her sister.

Like the time when Survivor had busted Dricka's nose for stealing her food and giving it to one of her friends, even after Survivor had bought all of them something to eat.

The fight was a brutal one!

The sisters went toe to toe, and blow for blow, for the first couple of minutes. But the agility and quickness of Survivor's hand speed proved to be a little too much for her older sister's wild swings, and slightly robust frame.

She left Dricka gasping for air upon every missed punch as Survivor connected with every countering blow until the fight was finally brought to a halt by a slew of other family members and friends. That only seemed to have increased their anger to its highest degree.

Angry sentiments from both siblings continued to escape their mouths with the most vicious of intentions only to be stopped by the aggressive slaps of Grandma Clifton and Mrs. B. Lee. They proudly took the liberty of trying to simultaneously smack the disrespect right back down the filthy and foul sounding throats of both willing participants. Dricka and Survivor definitely knew better.

The words stopped immediately. But the feelings did not! And the silence between the two sisters existed for months. Maybe even years possibly. Except for when in the presence of their elders. But even then, there were still little to almost no emotions involved. This always ignited several other quarrels between the two but just never in the presence of their older relatives.

As Dricka thought about her own issues, she thought maybe this was partially why Liz currently felt the way that she did towards Talent as well.

Maybe... Just maybe, Liz had inherited her mother's resentment and hatred towards her sister back in the day, from the womb.

All in hopes of possibly someday repaying the favor... even if it was to her precious little niece Talent. As the saying goes, "All is fair in love and war!"

Especially in War!

The mother-daughter religiously believed.

Chapter 16

So many different things were transpiring at the time within the Clifton family. And no matter how much prayer was being lifted up on her relative's behalf, things only appeared to be getting worse, Grandma Clifton thought to herself. She crouched down into an even lower position than she already was to resume her usual talk with God. She got lower just in case that particular stance wasn't submissive enough for her request to be acknowledged.

She needed God to listen to her more than ever at this point. Grandma Clifton could clearly see that the devil was working on her family by the chaos that he was currently creating amongst them.

Starting with Talent and Liz. Then, with her great grandson Potential, followed by her son-in-law, Big John. And now possibly with Survivor and Dricka all over again. She knew that it wouldn't take much at all to help reignite that flame, especially since it had never truly fizzled out.

Grandma Clifton felt another massive headache coming on. She knew it could possibly be due to the increase of her blood pressure. She also knew that her typical BC goodie powder would not be strong enough to help obliterate the oncoming pain. For the first time after many years, she seriously contemplated taking a drink.

A really, stiff drink at that!

Stooping so low now that she was almost laying directly flat on her face, she steadily poured her heart out to God. She could feel the negative energies from whatever sources in which they were currently evolving, constantly trying to draw her into its strongholds at the moment even while she was in the midst of praying.

Turning her hands palm-side upwards she stretched out even further across her bedroom floor in hopes of somehow receiving more additional strength than she was previously dealing with at the time within her natural being. The scriptures of Ephesians chapter six, starting at verse eleven, instantly began giving Grandma Clifton all of the strength that she would ever require.

At that moment, it was as if she could actually hear the Apostle Paul's words being spoken to her, vividly telling Grandma Clifton to equip herself with the full armor of God, that she may be able to stand against the wiles of the devil. And from that point forward, that's exactly what she began to do.

She quoted scripture after scripture to herself as if her life currently depended on it, which in a sense, it did, she presumed. She remembered just how cool, calm, and collected Jesus had reacted towards Satan when even He, Himself was being tempted by the devil in the book of Matthews, chapter 4 verses 1 through 11.

With that in mind, Grandma Clifton utilized God's word as her sword, cutting and slicing away every unhealthy and unfit thought that "the tempter" was sending her way until he was completely defeated and had fled away for the time being. For now, he was defeated, only to try and catch her at another one of her most vulnerable moments, just as he had done today. But Grandma Clifton swore to be better prepared.

For now, the battle with her was over. But, not for her family, Grandma Clifton was sure. She instantly made a mental note to advise them all on what was to come in hopes that each of them would or could equip themselves in that same exact manner. If Grandma Clifton didn't know anything else about "the tempter," as the bible also referred to him in the book of Matthews as well, she definitely understood that he would use any and everybody that he possibly could in order to completely destroy a thing.

Especially a family!

Grandma Clifton also knew that two of her very own descendants would possibly be more than willing to comply with him for the sake of revenge, too.

She picked up the phone in order to place a much-needed call to her extended family members on the other side of town, "The McCreary's." Just in case she needed some added reinforcements, Grandma Clifton thought.

Totally unaware of the fact that even they, themselves would soon be undergoing a serious battle of their own with "the tempter" as well, just as soon as "The Occupant" put the finishing touches of his plan into motion...

All starting with that no good, back-stabbing, highly- publicized, and newly glamorized, negro ophthalmologist, Dr. Wiseman!

Chapter 17

The temperament of "The Occupant's" mindset could be described as delusional. With every fleeting thought of Dr. Wiseman, or the McCreary's, "The Occupants" obsession towards them only seemed to magnify due to the many, days, weeks, and months of consistent man hours that had tirelessly been put into professionally tracking both parties every move. Like that of a private investigator, as "The Occupant," now praised themselves as being. Especially after tailing Officer Long and his partner the entire time that Big John's assault case was going on, never to be detected, of course.

"Not even by cop! Or should I say, by the long arms of the Law!" He confidently expressed speaking out loud within the four sparsely tainted walls in which, "The Occupant," resided. Giving the home the appearance of some type of medieval dungeon, in which, was almost impossible to adjust to your current surroundings. Especially, from the repetitive flickering of the dimly lit bulbs.

Magazine clippings and newspaper articles of all sorts were strewn all over the place. Completely covering almost every inch of the blotched floor in circumference resembling the aftereffects of a city that had recently just been hit by a massive tornado or hurricane. Better yet, by a substantially filthy, hoarder type individual. Which, in a lot of ways, definitely defined the likes and characteristics of "The Occupant," who didn't care one bit.

All that solely concerned "The Occupant" at that present time was the revenge that they felt they were due. And, with each passing moment that had not happened to Dr. Wiseman, or any of the McCreary's, "The Occupant" felt like a total failure. Which only seemed to inflame them even more.

"The Occupant" was a master of disguise, amongst a multitude of many other things. All of which had seemed to manifest within them at an early age. Especially with them being an only child. Never once did they believe in their wildest dreams that they would ever have the opportunity of finally bringing some of those make-believe childhood characters to life.

And, boy, were there a lot of them, "The Occupant" thought to themselves while doing everything that they could to somehow mask the current elation that just so happened to be over-taking their once extremely subtle and extensively poise demeanor.

Elation wasn't an emotion that was commonly felt from "The Occupant's" perspective. But, beatings, isolation, and mistreatment, definitely was. That was partially why they were still so very accustomed to living in that same type of manner as of currently. Books, newspapers, and magazines of all kinds had become their number one resource to the outside world and keeping "The Occupant" abreast to what was happening at all times. But it was also their way of becoming privy to the when's, why's, what's, and even where's of societies most popularized and most frequented tourist attractions.

"The Occupant" was a socialite within their own mind. And they didn't need the validation of anyone else to verify these facts for them at all. With all their newfound knowledge, style, and personalities, they had somehow even manipulated their way into the medical field where they had been practicing for almost a decade by falsifying a few documents here, a few other documents there. A medical exam here, and a medical exam there. Then Boom! Before you knew it, "The Occupant" was a certified physician. With the ability to practice medicine throughout all fifty states and even abroad.

"The Occupant" thought about their accomplishments for a moment. They were someone who had never actually stepped foot on any college campus or institution of any kind in order to become a certified physician but was now unknowingly responsible with the lives of thousands. "The Occupant" sadistically laughed to themselves.

"The Occupant" smiling ever so broadly in the mirror now, while enjoying the individual that was staring back at them with the fear of God plastered upon their once extremely attractive, but now, badly battered and almost unrecognizable face.

Dr. Wiseman, The McCreary's highly glamorized ophthalmologist, sat bound and gagged to the twin-size, prison-like bunk, with his arms outstretched, wrist and ankles restricted with rope, pleading for dear life with his eyes.

While "The Occupant" laughed the exact same laugh that they had been laughing while pulling away from the hospital, just before making the right turn on D. B. Todd Blvd. Only this time, it was filled with much more maliciousness!

"Aaahh ha ha ha ha ha! Aaaahhh ha ha ha ha haaa!

Chapter 18

The McCreary's had been waiting inside of Dr. Wiseman's office for almost thirty minutes to an hour now, and there had still been no sign of him at all. This was extremely uncommon for him, to say the least. Especially, since both he and the McCreary's were so adamant about promptness.

T. Thomas checked his wristwatch for a second time wondering what could possibly be prolonging Dr. Wiseman. Then, just as he was about to make his last and final trip up towards the receptionist desk to reschedule what in hopes would be their very last eye appointment, in walked a well-built, but slightly shorter Armenian looking doctor. They had the most intensive looking pair of no-nonsense type of eyes that either McCreary had ever seen.

The strange doctor politely spoke to the couple with much pleasantry in their voice. And, although kind, still, something about their voice alarmed the McCreary's, sending a cold chill right down the center of Mrs. Ida B's spine. This instinctively caused her to retract. She tightly grasped her husband's hand to confirm with herself that she was protected.

The McCreary's closely watched the stranger with much skepticism. The new doctor did everything within their power to help lower the defenses of the McCreary's. But no matter how hard they tried, the couple was not budging.

There was something completely odd about the strange doctor's actions. Something that just wasn't sitting well with the McCreary's at all. Something they both could feel. The hairs from both of their arms simultaneously stood at attention around the exact same time that the doctor began to speak. There was also something mysteriously disturbing about their eyes.

Picking up on the apprehension of the McCreary's, the stranger decided to take a completely different approach altogether. The doctor never once mentioned anything about Dr. Wiseman in order to help alleviate whatever distrust issues that already existed between them. And possibly in hopes of further annihilating some of the previous barriers that the husband-wife duo had set in place to protect themselves. They also knew that they happened to be connected to some very important people.

This was not going to be easy, thought the stranger. *But it was definitely doable.*

The strange doctor entered into the second phase of their plan, which from their perspective was almost guaranteed to work. Especially, after realizing just how loyal and devoted that the McCreary's were to their Lord and Savior, Jesus Christ. The very same Jesus that the doctor planned on using to carry out the last and final phase of their plan. *Which would definitely be the absolute best part of it all,* the strange doctor smiled while accidentally releasing a small chuckle. They quickly disguised the chuckle as if it were a cough, and covered their face with the clipboard that was within their hand as they falsely examined the so-called medical history of the McCreary's getting back to the business at hand. The doctor had definitely come entirely too far to fail.

The doctor finally restructuring their emotions but still under the watchful eye of the McCreary's. The strange doctor played the entire situation as smooth and as cool as Marvin Gaye's voice, delivering some of the test results with a sure flare of confidence. But definitely not them all so that they themselves could actually do all of the rescheduling for the McCreary's this time around. *Only this time it wouldn't be a doctor's appointment at all,* the extremely strange doctor thought to themselves with another covered smile.

The doctor instantly became overly nice to the McCreary's once again before casually ushering them out of the office and to the receptionist desk to someone that they knew that the McCreary's were familiar with when it came to answering or asking certain questions. But also, someone who had now been strategically manipulated and lured into the strange doctor's deceitful web of lies by the influence of money, the doctor deviously thought to themselves.

Once alone, the doctor removed the lab coat, the whitish-gray looking wig, the bushy mustache and goatee style beard, replacing it with something else entirely different in order to make it to their next scheduled appointment with one of the Clifton family's very own and pretty much newly inducted enemies, who for the time being "The Occupant" decided to keep disclosed.

They quickly accelerated their vehicle through traffic, in hopes of getting to the meeting ahead of schedule just to peep out the scene. They knew for a fact that you could never be too prepared. *Especially while dealing with heathens!* thought "The Occupant."

Chapter 19

Potential was still blatantly struggling with the whole entire shooting incident. But, nowhere near as much as before, except for when his breathing would become a bit labored by performing certain tasks that at one point and time had been extremely easy for him to do. Potential could feel a strong sense of self-doubt constantly sneaking into his thought process as he defensively willed himself forward.

He was gaining the strength he needed by vividly remembering all of the devastating, and highly immoral acts that his ancestor's had consistently battled against all throughout the history of this country's existence. Something that he never should've had to acknowledge or do at his age. Especially, not for just being BLACK!

Life would never be the same for Potential. Each of his existing scars would always display this for him. Looking down upon his skin, placing his finger into one of his wounds, he wondered how something so beautiful could possibly be so feared by so many other ethnicities. Imagining if this is what the disciple Thomas felt when touching the wounds of Jesus after He had risen due to his unbelief.

Potential avidly studied more than ever now, becoming all the more balanced within his everyday life, due to the proper guidance of his grandfather. But neither Big John, nor could any other active member of the Clifton family, change Potential's narrative when it came to that of Officer Long.

Every labored or shortened breath that Potential took, either while running, jumping, laughing, playing, or just merely standing around at times, only seemed to add to Potential's disgust even more.

Since the incident, Officer Long had been fired from the MNPD's police department without the ability of receiving his pension, due to his previous involvements in a highly scrutinized prostitution sting. Government officials of all ranks were now being questioned or investigated because of their corruption.

The news was more than gratifying to the Clifton family, but still not enough to appease

Potential's damaged heart. From his perspective, Officer Long and his partner should've been punished far more severely for their actions.

Potential tried his best not to entertain certain thoughts within his young mind, because he fully understood that they were totally against God's will. And the last thing that Potential had ever wanted to be towards God was disobedient. But, yet and still, his thoughts towards the entire situation had never changed. So much so that even Potential's prayer didn't seem to be working at the moment. But did Potential really want them to, he guiltily thought to himself.

Potential made his way outdoors, because, being trapped inside of the house was causing him to think entirely too much. Especially when most of those thoughts were negative.

Unbeknownst to Potential, far across town, Officer Long was somewhere sadly covered in puke and liquor. He was dwelling in the darkened basement of what was now his currently foreclosed home, feeling the exact same way, in a sense, but far worse.

The chrome-plated, double-action revolver, comfortably lay within Officer Long's stubby little hand. He professionally cocked and un-cocked the hammer of this monstrous tool on more than several different occasions after the completion of him cleaning it. Truthfully loving the sound of the dangerous mechanism's rhythmic click... click... clicking. Almost more than the traumatizing boom that followed the clicking noise after being discharged.

Maniacally thinking to himself, in a very deranged type of manner, just how good it would actually feel to finally hear that life altering click... click... boom, once again.

Chapter 20

Dr. Wiseman struggled against his restraints with all of his might. But the sliding knot that "The Occupant" had masterfully administered seemed almost impossible for him to unravel, nor loosen. Dr. Wiseman had done almost everything he could think of in order to get free.

He shifted his weight from side to side while twisting his body in some unpleasant positions in hopes of creating the leeway that he so desperately needed in order to finally pull himself free. Despite all of Dr. Wiseman's efforts, none of them proved to be successful.

The constant buildup of his current frustration aligned with the fatigue of his rapidly declining muscles along with his slowly deteriorating mindset, all seemed to be leading Dr. Wiseman closer and closer to the jagged cliffs of defeat and possibly over the edge if he didn't figure out something quick.

Racking his brain for solutions, Dr. Wiseman could only think of two things that he could willingly do at the time. Take some very much needed deep breaths in order to help calm his nerves and pray. So, pray he did.

He acknowledged just how imperative that prayer had always been to him throughout the course of his entire life. So how could he not implement it now during one of his most difficult times of need, Dr. Wiseman thought to himself.

The oh so simple, but yet, very powerful words of his prayer effortlessly began to flow from his heart, instantly gracing the ears of his Lord and Savior, Jesus Christ. He not only had been Dr. Wiseman's strength over the years, but, also his entire backbone from the very moment that his mother had ever taught him to pray as a child.

Comfortably poising himself while steadily doing his best to regain sole control of his excessively palpitating heartbeat, Dr. Wiseman battled against time. He knew that time was of an essence because the whack-job referred to as "The Occupant," would surely be returning soon.

It had been a little over a week or so since Dr. Wiseman's abduction. Maybe a day or two less, give or take due to the many sunsets that he'd counted from the small rectangular plexiglass window that adorned the wall that was opposite of the door.

The foul-smelling stench of the bucket's contents, that had become Dr. Wiseman's toilet, smelled. It was on the brink of overflowing. Several of the yellowish-brown like fluids had already aggressively found its way to the articled covered floor making the headlines in which they'd currently taken their rest upon totally unrecognizable.

Flies, gnats, and many other different types of coprophagous insects emerged from the bucket's interior in droves of hundreds contaminating everything within reach. Even Dr. Wiseman was covered in the insects. He shook, twisted, bounced, hollered, and screamed doing everything within his power to keep the insects out of his personal space. His screams were muffled by an extremely moistened and discolored gag.

Anger rested in Dr. Wiseman's eyes as his body filled with rage, passionately pushing him to fight against his restraints even more, especially after hearing a voice. It wasn't the common everyday type of voice that he'd heard throughout the hospital on a day-to-day basis. Nor was it one that he could fully familiarize with either. But, yet and still, it was there. He had to give it everything that he possibly could in order to get their attention.

He summoned from deep within him an indescribable strength that had never presented itself to Dr. Wiseman before, until that very moment. It was deeper than fight or flight because in Dr. Wiseman's current predicament, running was no longer an option for him.

No! This was live or die!

And the latter of the two words is what must have initially sparked something within Dr. Wiseman to respond so vigilantly. Never in the existence of his adult life had he ever envisioned perishing from God's great creation until that very moment. If that were going to be the case, it definitely wasn't going to be as simple, or as easy, as he'd made it for "The Occupant" up until that point, Dr. Wiseman assured himself.

He instantly felt another strong bout of falsified fear slowly disguising itself in the forms of anxiety, casually easing itself completely down Dr. Wiseman's spinal cord, and all the way into the depths of his spleen. It momentarily, paralyzed all previously functioning body parts. He continuously performed several different types of breathing techniques to help redirect his temporary train of thought.

In and out... in and out... in and out! Dr. Wiseman inhaled and exhaled, desperately trying to regain control of his breathing, while pondering on his next move. The voice that he thought he heard earlier appeared to be drawing closer and closer with each passing breath.

He was totally unaware of the fact that it was his very own subconscious attentively trying to pre-warn Dr. Wiseman to take a closer look at the restraints of his left wrist. The restraints had somehow almost wiggled itself completely free of its binding loop. Furthermore, making it impossible to cinch or tighten towards any kind of resistance, as it had before. But from the current looks of things, Dr. Wiseman wouldn't be figuring that part out anytime soon. Especially now that "The Occupant" had once again returned.

Chapter 21

"The Occupant" entered the room with the same devious smile as before exiting the premises earlier that day. But it was quickly replaced by a frown that was so maliciously motivated due to the extremely pungent and foul-smelling odor that had greeted their nostrils as they quickly shoved open the wrought iron door. The sudden stream of funk almost lifted "The Occupant" completely off their feet in a moment's instance. It was only because of the sturdiness of the door frame that they were able to maintain balance.

Bile surfaced from the depths of "The Occupant's" stomach in an instant due to the abnormally wretched stench. Having somewhat of a weak digestive system pertaining to such things, "The Occupant" was unable to contain it. Large globs of spit, along with many other different types of disgusting fragments embraced the floor adding even more unfathomable substances to the already horrendous environment.

It instantly roused up anger within 'The Occupant" that was only bridled by the room's disheartening stench. They once again slammed the huge, abnormally heavy, ironed door giving Dr. Wiseman a bit more time to contemplate his next move.

Steadily puking up their insides from the other side of the door, "The Occupant" was more furious than ever. Madder than an angry pack of yellow jackets, who's nest had been tampered with, or completely plucked from its spot. Even more upset than they had been after figuring out that the McCreary's were no longer considering them as an option in performing their eye surgery, but instead, had deceptively chosen Dr. Wiseman, the so-called, African American doctor, over a technically privileged, much lighter skin-tone having, American-born citizen such as themselves. To "The Occupant," this was considered to be more than the ultimate act of betrayal by mostly all real Americanized standards.

They hurriedly scampered away from the door in search of obtaining a Vicks vapor rub type substance to apply to and underneath their nostrils in order to help desensitize the smell. To "The Occupant," there was no way on earth that they would wait a moment longer in dispensing their vengeance.

Savagely rummaging through the contents of their extremely cluttered and disturbingly messy living quarters, "The Occupant" finally stumbled across what it was that they were looking for. Quickly applying the very peculiar smelling cream onto their skin, they were more than ready to finally administer every single ounce of pain that they believed Dr. Wiseman so truly deserved. "The Occupant" sadistically thought about every aspect of vengeance as they rapidly scurried back to where they had come from like the malevolent little rodent they appeared to be.

As the devilish snarl openly revealed the multi-layered row of bottom teeth that existed within "The Occupant's" mouth, it added to the ideal resemblance of the hideous scavenger in which they were previously being compared.

Feelings of satisfaction were once again arising within "The Occupant." As he approached the door with a newly empowered energy confidently emitting from their pores, "The Occupant" placed their hand upon the doorknob to re-enter the room and that's when it dawned on them.

In the midst of everything that was happening, "The Occupant" suddenly remembered that they had somehow forgotten their most praiseworthy possessions. They cautiously stepped away from the huge, wrought-iron door, for a second time, in order to retrieve their meticulously sharpened, custom-made suturing kit. It contained some of the most diabolical and sought-after instruments known to man. Tools that hadn't been seen or used since the very unethical days and times of Dr. J. Marion Sims.

Dr. J. Marion Sims was the so-called "Father of Modern Gynecology," as he was named at one point by American society. He was given this title even though it was factually known that he was using enslaved Black women as constant guinea pigs or test subjects without giving them anesthesia between the years of 1845 to 1849, in order to further increase his knowledge within the medical field. He performed over thirty procedures on one particularly enslaved Black woman who, only by the grace of God, actually survived them all.

That is exactly what "The Occupant" planned on doing to Dr. Wiseman. Using him as their very own modern day guinea pig, or personalized testing dummy.

But "The Occupant" wouldn't be trying to discover anything new about science at this point. No, they merely just wanted to know how loud Dr. Wiseman could scream, and for how long he could withstand certain types of pain once the torturing process had begun.

Chapter 22

Re-entering the room with the excitement of a child on Christmas day, "The Occupant" arrogantly proceeded forward without a single, solitary care in the world. Totally unaware of the apparent dangers that silently awaited them on the other side.

Dr. Wiseman had finally become calm enough to suddenly hear himself think. He feverishly began maneuvering his left wrist in a manner that seemed to be awkwardly uncomfortable for him. It appeared that he had somehow dislocated several of the eight carpal bones within his wrist. Possibly the scaphoid, lunate, and trapezium to be exact. But, nonetheless, or regardless of how it all transpired, the rope that had currently held Dr. Wiseman hostage for so many long and arduous days was no longer intact, leaving one of his previously constricted body parts absolutely free.

For Dr. Wiseman, this was a complete miracle to say the obvious. He untied his remaining limbs with a quickness that couldn't be captured by the most accurate of clocks. He instinctively massaged and stretched his extremely taut muscles in hopes of desperately bringing forth some much-needed circulation to the most excruciating parts of his upper and lower extremities.

The stiffness that Dr. Wiseman was experiencing felt somewhat paralyzing. That feeling was short-lived and had quickly dissolved after acknowledging the turning of the doorknob followed by an aggressive push. As their eyes instantly locked on one another, they both were totally caught off guard for a moment or two. Both sets of eyes narrowed into tight little slits while taking another second or two more to fully comprehend what was happening.

Just like two ferocious animals from the wild, both parties propelled forward attacking one another with a vengeance that was indescribable. Fist and feet flew from every possible direction known to man. Most of them solidly connected with the uttermost of viciousness as they both desperately did everything within their power, trying to take the other out. But since simple mathematics wasn't a part of this extremely difficult situation, then you know for a fact that this would definitely not be the case in the matter.

"The Occupant," although a smidgen smaller in size, definitely made up for that with a blinding quickness as they steadily swayed from side to side, simultaneously bouncing from foot to foot in the confined space. They were arrogantly showing off their Muay Thai - Taekwondo fighting skills, all the while, throwing blow after blow, and kick after kick from what appeared to be the most impossible positions. Several blows accurately landed somewhere flush onto Dr. Wiseman's visually weakened frame, instinctually evaporating even more of his almost completely spent energy level.

This left him unsuccessfully trying to figure out a solution on how to properly defend himself. At that moment, it confusingly seemed to be a little too difficult of an equation for Dr. Wiseman to solve.

"The Occupant's" fighting style was unorthodox. Very unorthodox to be exact. Like that of the great Anderson Silva, Jon Jones, Michael Page, or Michel Pereira. Making it even that much more difficult for Dr. Wiseman to target, focus on, or truly adjust. Upon acknowledging the doctor's previous perplexities, "The Occupant" began showboating their talents even more, loving every single moment of it as they gladly witnessed the huge, discolored lump that now currently resided underneath Dr. Wiseman's left eye as it continued to swell in size. Without showing the least bit of mercy, they continuously directed every punch towards its projected target with the utmost of worst intentions while gleefully watching it completely close.

It was in the midst of all of "The Occupant's" previous celebrations that the tables suddenly turned. Just as they had done for Big John Tate, former Tennessee heavyweight champion of the world. With only forty-five seconds remaining in the last round, he began to go against his trainers' instructions by celebrating and opening up to the chants and cheers of the crowd, catching a huge left hand from opponent Mike Weaver, that not only left Big John Tate delirious, but that had also cost him his title as well. In a sense, this is exactly what happened to "The Occupant" as the powerful right hook of Dr. Wiseman's damaging blow cleanly connected to the left side of "The Occupant's" temple, driving them several feet backwards, as they drunkenly fought to remain in an upright position. With nothing else able to assist them but the feces-filled bucket which had been toppled over upon first touch of impact. "The Occupant" was instantly covered from chest to legs.

Chapter 23

Trying to become better acclimated with his current surroundings, while constantly gagging up what seemed to be his lungs from the gruesome scene, Dr. Wiseman had become extremely light-headed. "The Occupant" seized the brief opportunity in between his assault to finally make an escape. They desperately scrambled through the poisonous excrements, without fully making it to their feet but still moving just well enough in order to get to the huge, wrought-iron door, before Dr. Wiseman could even attempt to give chase.

Dr. Wiseman, clumsily slipping and sliding through the toxic sludge, had accurate vision out of one good eye, and was still able to perform just well enough to get a hand on the slithering varmint. But he was only able to rip the pocket from their coat leaving some extremely beneficial, but also, some very disturbing information behind.

In that moment, Dr. Wiseman was forced to make a huge decision about the contents that were now scattered all throughout the waste covered floor. He had no other choice but to gather it all up by hand when he visibly witnessed several different photographs of, he and the McCreary's, along with several other members of the Clifton family. But what stood out to Dr. Wiseman and was the strangest discovery out of everything that had been found, was the MNPD card belonging to an Officer Long.

"Officer Long... Officer Long... where do I know this name from?" Dr. Wiseman questioned, unable to come up with the answer in that moment. He finally made his way out of the door, closely observing the oh so familiar scene, when it dawned on him that he was somewhere close to the hospital's boiling room area.

"What the...!" Dr. Wiseman surprisingly voiced. He collapsed to the floor in a very peculiar type of manner. The fall was shortly followed by a loud crack. Something was either broken or dislocated but definitely went unnoticed for the time being due to the fatigue that was currently attacking Dr. Wiseman's body, permitting him to scream or call out for help.

Chapter 24

Fully awake, but still unable to move, Dr. Wiseman fearfully watched the huge rodents draw closer and closer to his body as he helplessly laid there somewhat paralyzed on the cold, moistened, concrete. Some of the rats were skeptical in the beginning. But not all. And for the ones that were not, they would soon give confidence to the others if Dr. Wiseman didn't do something and do it quickly.

Dr. Wiseman was an avid reader and had read many stories of how certain individuals from certain lifestyles would discontinue some of the worst of their enemies by either dropping their bodies into hollowed caves or other abandoned and run-down places, like the Farallon Islands, which was located approximately 28 miles from the Golden Gate Bridge, with several open wounds or deep abrasions, so that the blood could smell. All in hopes of leaving behind little to no possible remains for identification purposes of any kind just in case the body was somehow mysteriously stumbled upon.

Growing up in the housing projects of Preston Taylor Homes where some of those very same scavengers of the night grew to be so huge in size that even the toughest of alley-cats wouldn't attempt to contest them. Not even when two against one. Dr. Wiseman figuratively assumed that being fully consumed by the likes of what was currently manifesting right before his very own eyes, shouldn't or wouldn't be impossible for them to do. Especially, when some of the rodents that were standing before him were the size of beavers, extending more than 2 feet long when including their tail.

Deliriousness was a definite understatement in defining Dr. Wiseman's mindset at the moment. Looking into the beady, black, eyes of the hungry, disease-carrying, omnivores that preferred meat in this instance, only magnified his terror a hundred-fold.

Dr. Wiseman intelligently knew that he had to move and move quickly! Because, if he did not, these newly inspired carnivorous creatures that were even closer to him in proximity now, were about to feed. And he would definitely be the prey.

Some added strength had re-entered Dr. Wiseman's body, but still not enough to scare them away. He could certainly feel various places of his body being tugged at, and the feces-covered garments that he was enmeshed in, wasn't making things any better for him, Dr. Wiseman bewilderingly thought.

As the fear of possibly being eaten alive was becoming more and more of a reality for him, Dr. Wiseman traumatically watched and listened to the determined creatures constantly gnashing and ripping at his clothes, desperately trying to sink those hideous looking teeth of theirs into any parts of Dr. Wiseman's melanated skin to taste the richness of his priceless blood.

Dr. Wiseman made another conscious effort of screaming and moving his body to ward off any possible dangers that the rodents could cause. But his lungs and limbs were still too weakened to accomplish the task. This only seemed to infuriate the savages even more, as the creature's aggressiveness instantly escalated to a new level. They snatched, pulled, and shredded Dr. Wiseman's garments as if they were somehow communicating, doing their absolute best to take full advantage of the opportunity that lay before them.

The silent squeaking of the abnormal varmints were no longer present, and had now been replaced by very deep, gut-wrenching snarls, like that of a dog. A very massive and aggressive dog! Something as vicious as a Rottweiler.

This terrified Dr. Wiseman more than ever as the beady, black, eyes of the rodents transformed into solid red embers of burning hot coals appearing to multiply by the seconds. Their eyes vividly illuminated the small boiling room area like the inside of a volcano that was about to erupt.

The sparseness of Dr. Wiseman's breathing was more than noticeable to the rodents, and he could also feel a wetness seeping from somewhere beneath his waistline. Upon first thought, he assumed it to be urine. But that's when he smelled it. The stench of Blood! His Blood!

Dr. Wiseman shook his head in defeat.

The vicious varmints had finally become successful. Dr. Wiseman suddenly rationalized and knew that it would only be a matter of time before it was completely over for him. Shedding a tear at the fact that his life would end so unintentionally meaningless, he put up another final attempt to scream and fight the creatures off. But still nothing happened.

It was over! He was over! Dr. Wiseman embarrassingly admitted.

He closed his eyes to say his last and final prayer to his Lord and Savior, Jesus Christ, in hopes of somehow making his last remaining breaths here on earth extremely peaceful. The savages slowly backed away just a little, as if out of respect for what he was about to do, before finally finishing him off, Dr. Wiseman thought.

He was totally unaware of the fact that his life was currently being saved by the janitor in the Dunn's Janitorial shirt, who had frustratingly pushed open the door looking for some of the company's misplaced materials.

Chapter 25

Pandemonium was rapidly spreading throughout the families, and no one was being spared. "The Occupant" sat ducked off across the street from the McCreary's home waiting for an opportunity to rapidly make their move.

The conversation with Officer Long had been short-lived and sort of rushed, due to the foul up that had recently transpired earlier between them and Dr. Wiseman. In order to prevent the next phase of their plan from going astray, "The Occupant" knew that they had to move strategically.

"The Occupant" cursed themselves more than a thousand times over once again for losing the very vital information that had been safely tucked deeply within the pocket of their lab coat. They swore in all seriousness to physically repay Dr. Wiseman back yet again, for somehow disassembling everything that supposedly could've been great when pertaining to "The Occupant's" plan.

Watching the McCreary's respond so lovingly to one another almost made "The Occupant" lose the contents of their stomach for a second time, as they hurriedly took a huge gulp of the warm, watered-down ginger ale that had been left in the cupholder of their vehicle earlier that day.

"Sss Pitooey!" "The Occupant" vehemently spat, quickly extracting the acid less soda from their mouth in the harshest of fashions, while spewing the sugary substance all over the windshield, dashboard, and steering wheel of the vehicle. Instantly ticking them off even more.

"Really? Really? You ruined my drink too!" The Occupant psychotically yelled blaming Dr. Wiseman and the McCreary's for this as well. They furiously crushed the can in the palm of their hand, as the contents spilled all over the carpet.

Simmering with anger, "The Occupant" searched their body for the handkerchief that normally resided in the left pocket of their polo shirt. But surprisingly enough, even that was gone. Violent screams erupted loudly from "The Occupant's" mouth before aiming their frustration towards the steering wheel, and dashboard area of the vehicle, until hearing the obnoxious blaring of a horn. This rapidly sent "The Occupant" crouching for cover to prevent from being seen.

"The Occupant" remained slouched down in the front seat of the vehicle for at least twenty minutes. Still hesitant of checking out the scenery, fearing someone was possibly watching the strange sedan, if not the entire neighborhood, making them feel more and more like the little coward that they obviously were with each passing moment.

"What are you doing? Get it together you wuss!" "The Occupant" angrily stated to themselves in disbelief. But still never making a move. They were hoping that Officer Long was having some much better luck with the Clifton's on the other side of town.

He was totally oblivious to the fact that the ex-officer, whom "The Occupant" had currently partnered up with, was now being held at gunpoint in a darkened alley somewhere off of 40th avenue, by Big John and a couple of his brothers.

Guess who was holding the gun?

Potential!

His eyes were steady, and totally relaxed, while showing a small hint of that crooked smile that would someday down the line become one of the most attractive attributes from his many pleasant features, as he enjoyably watched his grandfather forcibly remove Officer Long from the unauthorized sedan.

Chapter 26

Potential watched the scene from a short distance away.

Officer Long kicked, screamed, and desperately clawed at the seats of the sedan in hopes of not being fully extracted from the vehicle. But he only made the matter more severe for himself causing Big John, Frank Nitty, and Uncle Gee to all grasp different parts of the ex-officer's body, harshly harpooning him completely from the car. His body took a slight bounce off the hard, pebbled-filled, pavement. A disturbing snapping sound was heard that was far less painful than it actually appeared.

Potential smirked at the grimacing face of the ex-officer before taking a step closer in his direction. He attentively watched as his much older relatives filled Officer Long's body with several deafening blows, hitting him with a weird looking black leather, bar-like, object. Potential would later find out that the weapon was a slap jack, something that the military and policemen both sometimes used as a weapon to administer even more damaging pain to their victims, or commonly targeted opposition.

The pleadings were a bit unnerving for Potential in the beginning, but quite gratifying as well.

The memories of Officer Long sitting on the witness stand, blatantly lying about how Big John and Talent were solely responsible for the entire incident that had taken place at Florine Cowan Academy, had once again resurfaced into Potential's mind. Potential remembered him doing everything within his unrighteous heart to get them both convicted. The lashings to Officer Long's body furthermore continued until the much older gentlemen of his family had finally become fatigued.

Still gripping the weapon within his hands, while reiterating the many lies that were professed to the courts from Officer Long's perspective, really placed a very disgusting taste in Potential's mouth. A taste that could only be quenched or resolved by a certain act of cruelty, Potential believed.

The older gentlemen of his family sat back, closely observing their young cub arduously wrestling with his next decision. Potential's finger carefully teased the deadly mechanism's extremely sensitive hair-trigger. But still, no one intervened.

The mood had drastically shifted from life to death in the blink of an eye, and Potential was currently in charge of its fate. Big John slowly inched his body towards his grandson, being meticulously careful not to startle him, or make any sudden moves.

Big John could visibly see the death in Potential's eyes and knew that he had what it took to pull the trigger. And so did the others. Especially Officer Long who was now begging and pleading more than ever before. His face and eyes were full of tears and mucus as they embarrassingly fell onto the front of his shirt. Potential cold-heartedly stared at him in disbelief.

Officer Long profusely sobbed like that of a battered child. "Please young man! Please! Please. Don't. Do. This! From the bottom of my heart, I'm Sorry! Potential, I'm begging you! Please! I AM SO SORRY!"

He realized at that very moment just how bad he wanted to live and not die. Especially not so violently, Officer Long thought as he tightly closed his eyes. He begged God to intervene on his behalf in hopes that Potential would spare his life. His prayers must've slightly changed the atmosphere for Potential just a little, as a conversation that his mother had once shared with him about the McCreary's had suddenly re-entered his psyche.

Potential slowly began backing away from Officer Long. His finger was still firmly positioned on the hair-trigger due to his indecisiveness. When attempting to finally hand the weapon over to his grandfather, Officer Long heroically tried reaching for Potential's leg.

Click… Click… BOOM!

The dangerous mechanism violently exploded as it hit the ground sending everyone scrambling for cover. Except for one who surprisingly remained emotionless as they steadily stared at the smoking gun, faintly whispering to an unknown entity while instinctively clutching their wound.

Chapter 27

"Nooooo!" Potential screamed at the top of his lungs as he fearfully watched his loved one slowly slumping forward. Frank Nitty quickly dashed towards his sibling in a motion-picture type of running style in order to give his brother some assistance. Frank screamed and prayed the entire time that he was in route, dodging and maneuvering around certain people in order to finally get to him.

Totally taken aback by the sudden occurrences, Big John stood frozen for a brief moment with his mouth ajar. He was unable to properly react and was surprisingly looking around trying to figure out what had actually happened. Frank Nitty carefully coddled his brother's body within his arms, slowly removing Uncle Gee's hands from his midsection area in order to better assess the wound. He was hoping that all of the medical training that he had once received during combat was still currently up to par.

Uncle Gee was somewhat incoherent and a tad bit delusional from the impact. He excessively moaned as Frank Nitty summoned Big John over to assist him in straightening out his brother's lower extremities in hopes of making him more comfortable. Potential stood close by nervously awaiting Frank Nitty's next command, which would never come.

The two older gentlemen moved in unison. Delicately and deliberately as if they'd both dealt with situations such as this more than a thousand times. Big John carefully handed Frank Nitty some type of weird looking styptic powder that he'd quickly retrieved from the vehicle in order to help stanch the flow of blood.

Problem was there was no blood to be found, confusing Frank Nitty. He aggressively ripped Uncle Gee's shirt open with force, sending buttons haphazardly flying in every known direction, but with no specific destination. Everyone within striking distance either ducked for cover or shielded their eyes all in hopes of protecting their vision. Everyone except for Potential who stood closest to the ground because of his height.

"Man, there's no blood! I can't find any blood, man! Help me flip him over!" Frank Nitty fearfully screamed at Big John.

By this time, Big John seemed even more perplexed than he had previously been before. He bewilderingly leaned forward in order to get a better look, scanning and searching Uncle Gee's body for himself to see if Frank Nitty was telling the truth, which indeed he was.

He reached down to check Uncle Gee's pulse as it pulsated hard and strong on the tip of Big John's fingers like that of a physically fit teenager. Big John harshly pinched Uncle Gee's side, desperately trying to remove a piece of his flesh from his body if he was able to do so due to the unnecessary worry that he'd caused.

"Aaaarrgghh Man, what are you doing! I'm sitting here dying and you're constantly inflicting even more pain on me dude, where's my brother!" Uncle Gee barked trying his best to once again sound weakened, but the jig was up.

"Get up fool! Ain't nothing wrong with your crazy behind!" Big John aggressively shot back. He instantly pulled his relative from the pavement, as he more than aggressively dusted him off. Extremely grateful that Uncle Gee was alright, Big John continuously assaulted him with his huge hands.

"What! He's not shot! What do you mean, he's not shot?" Frank Nitty surprisingly yelled grateful himself as well, but still feigning to be extremely angry also.

"Well, if he's not shot then he's about to be! Because you literally scared the living daylights outta me dude. Now, hand me that shirt so I can cover up the front of my darn pants!" Frank Nitty embarrassingly laughed, as everyone else followed suit until recognizing that Officer Long was no longer present amongst them. He had somehow slithered away in the midst of all of the commotion. But Officer Long silently watched from what he hoped to be a secluded spot in some nearby bushes.

He angrily murmured to himself while breathing with a raspy tone through swollen lips, due to his fractured ribs, and visibly broken nose.

"You definitely haven't seen the last of me, you Clifton's, and that you can honestly believe!" Officer Long promised. He did his best not to make a sound as the huge, discolored snake menacingly stared him down as it cautiously made its way closer and closer to his hiding space.

Chapter 28

Several weeks had passed since the incident transpired involving Dr. Wiseman, Mrs. Ida B., T. Thomas, and the Clifton's. Although things were quiet at the moment, everyone was still on high alert. Especially Dr. Wiseman, who had diligently fought and battled to get his health back in order. He had just been cleared to finally return to work.

Returning to work was something that he'd been stressing about doing since being thoroughly examined and released from the hospital only days after being found semi-conscious on the boiling room floor. A place that he would never forget for as long as he lived.

The thought alone was simply traumatizing for him. It left him completely skeptical and paranoid of almost any and everything around him, which had the tendency of only unraveling his nerves even more.

After much deliberation, Dr. Wiseman undeniably concluded with himself that in order to become the amazing doctor that he had always envisioned himself someday becoming for the sake of his people, he was going to have to learn to finally get past all of what happened to him someday soon.

He constantly stared down at the metal object that he skeptically tucked deep into the corner of his gym bag and seriously contemplated on removing it altogether. He decided against it and hurriedly departed the doors of his home nervously clutching the bag extremely close to his body the entire time.

Dr. Wiseman gently eased the bag down onto the backseat of the vehicle as if it was some type of C4 explosive. He wiped beads of sweat from his brow while constantly peering through the rear-view mirror, just before entering onto the intersection.

He noticed a car, appearing to be an undercover cop car, slowly picking up momentum. Every time Dr. Wiseman switched lanes, so did they.

Dr. Wiseman nervously acknowledged that the car was staying just far enough behind him where they could not be recognized.

His heart was rapidly pounding within his chest as the strange, unmarked vehicle drifted to a moderate cruise, keeping a safe distance of no more than one or two cars between them at all times. Dr. Wiseman struggled to maintain control.

"Breathe! Breathe!" Dr. Wiseman desperately voiced to himself.

His lungs were seemingly drawing tighter and tighter with each abnormal attempt as he continuously inhaled and exhaled in deep successions, doing his best to remain focused on the road.

Chapter 29

Grandma Clifton sat quietly while watching her entire family from a distance. She closely observed every single individual that remained, from youngest to oldest, and was more than satisfied with almost every descendant of her stock. Both good and bad.

But none of them had given her more joyous moments than Talent and Potential. This truth, Grandma Clifton would sometimes openly admit after such small and simple tasks were performed, like the reading of her personal mail. That task could only be done by Talent from Grandma Clifton's perspective. She would always give a reason as to why she had always chosen Talent over the rest of her other grandchildren so that none of them would become too jealous.

Grandma Clifton always explained why supporting and investing in the future of their children was not only imperative for the entire family to do, but also why it would be extremely beneficial to each and every member that carried the Clifton name for years to come. Especially Survivor's children.

All of her descendants possessed some extremely special qualities. Qualities that had definitely allowed the family to continue to excel throughout the many struggles that life had constantly tossed their way over the years. But none of their gifts had ever shone more brightly than Talent and Potential's, Grandma Clifton admitted, desperately hoping that those of her relatives that couldn't quite understand her current logic at the time, someday eventually would.

Grandma Clifton's entire life had been based around sacrifice. Sacrifice for her late husband "Hen." Sacrifice for her entire family and friends. But none of it was more important to her than family. Her Family! Grandma Clifton would always seriously profess to every listening ear within her tribe, looking each and every last one of them directly in their eyes at one point or another, until finally completing her message. She let them all see just how serious she was about what she was saying.

Grandma Clifton knew she wouldn't always be around to help guide her loved ones. Whether they wanted to fully accept that fact or not, it was the truth and she needed them to be prepared.

In certain instances, Grandma Clifton didn't want to acknowledge certain aspects pertaining to death. She wished that she could live forever at times, which she knew was impossible. But her joy came from knowing that she would someday dwell in the house of her Lord and Savior, Jesus Christ, with the rest of her loved ones. Especially those that were slaves, as her mother and father had once been.

Grandma Clifton envisioned heaven in her dreams. Even sometimes when she was wide awake. The closest thing that she could possibly compare to heaven at that moment was what she was witnessing happen right underneath her very own roof, the gathering of her priceless family on a beautiful Saturday afternoon. The following day, right after the completion of Sunday service, they would all help out with cooking together as a family.

These were the moments that Grandma Clifton loved with all of her heart and soul. The people that were the remainder of her existing soul. She would not, nor could not, rest until they were all on one accord just as their ancestors had been years before, Grandma Clifton proudly reminisced.

Smiling from ear to ear, she surveyed the ins and outs of her moderately decorated living quarters with true admiration, until finally locking eyes with Liz. Her one and only troublesome grandchild that almost always seemed to defy the odds by repeatedly going against the rest of her family for whatever reasons. She acted just as her mother Dricka had also acted around that exact same age as well. At least until Grandma Clifton had finally put some personal get-right on her behind that even bleach couldn't remove.

It was looking as if she was going to have to do it again, Grandma Clifton thought to herself as she continued to caress the pearl-handle straight razor that was within her pocket until Liz had finally diverted her gaze in another direction, which just so happened to land on her cousin Talent.

Talent was the absolute last person on earth that Liz had ever wanted to see, and her disgusted facial expression clearly showed it. Grandma Clifton took full notice of her facial expression before disappointingly shaking her head.

"Like I always say, sometimes you just might have to beat the devil out of a few folks in order for them to learn their lesson, or so that they may receive their blessing," Grandma Clifton stated. "And that goes for family too!" She concluded.

She finally removed her hand from the pocket of her old, terrycloth, robe before tenderly pinching the chubby little cheeks of baby Samantha, the newest addition of Grandma Clifton's clan.

Chapter 30

Sensing that someone was watching her from behind, as the hairs on the nape of her neck stood at attention, Talent aggressively turned to confront her antagonist. She figured that she already knew exactly who it was, but to her surprise, this time it was not.

Liz was nowhere in sight. But the people that were, surprised her even more. Especially since they had no business ever showing their faces amongst her family again. Talent angrily stared into the deceitful eyes of Shica and Sheena without as much as a blink.

Talent closely observed the two disloyal friends with much skepticism, wondering how they and Liz had suddenly reconciled. But birds of a feather did flock together, so Talent was more than positive that slithering snakes had pretty much done the same.

The coldness that masked Talent's face was unreadable, like that of a professional poker player with a winning hand, constantly trying to bait in their opponent, as she half-heartedly reciprocated Shica and Sheena's greeting.

She was biting down on the inside of her lip until the saltiness of her very own blood was present, never once wincing from the pain. The taste of blood within her mouth ignited a spark within Talent that was almost uncontrollable. But, yet and still, she remained poised. She knew that they would be expecting some type of reaction from her in order for them to initiate their next move.

Afterall, this was chess, not checkers, Talent thought, and she was definitely the Queen!

The Queen was the only piece on the chessboard that was able to move any number of spaces, whether vertically, horizontally, or diagonally, giving her the combined power of both, rook and bishop. To some players, this made her even more powerful than the King.

In that moment, Talent knew exactly what moves she would have to make in order to completely obliterate the two imbeciles that stood before her. And she would do it with pleasure.

She smiled at Shica and Sheena both, while openly exposing her blood-stained teeth.

Chapter 31

Saturday eased by at a snail's pace after seeing Shica and Sheena, which had become somewhat of a distraction for Talent in a sense. The exact thing that Liz was hoping it would do as she secretly monitored her little cousin from the backseat of her mother's vehicle. She had suddenly disappeared to the vehicle after the stare down had blatantly taken place between her and Grandma Clifton.

Satisfaction adorned Liz's face from the discombobulation that she had currently caused her cousin. She always loved when she could change Talent's normal joyful mood into one of pure somberness from the ugliness of her actions.

This instantly gave Liz a small sense of victory. She deeply inhaled the stale, foul-smelling odor from the old cigarette smoke that had permanently ingrained itself within the seats of her mother's vehicle. But, yet and still, she smiled basking in the moment like a person who had previously accomplished one of their most important goals. She arrogantly clasped her hands behind her head while propping her feet upon the back of her mother's seat, resting her eyes.

Liz fantasized about Talent, but not in the way that a mentally sane person would. No, this time her thoughts were completely demented. Absolutely dysfunctional as a matter of fact. Just the way that Liz had preferred. Only this time, Talent's picture wasn't attached to some oversized stuffed animal. This time she was actually there, and Liz was beating on her with the most malicious of intentions.

Whaling away on Talent like an obsessed person, as Talent desperately tried defending her face by covering up with her forearms in order to divert some of the blows. This method proved to be pointless at the time and Liz evilly grinned.

The dream had become so real for Liz at this point that she could feel a great deal of the blows actually making contact with her very own body. Pain began shrieking from several different areas of her torso all the way up to her head.

Nightfall had suddenly overtaken the place of the sun, no longer permitting her to see. Liz's eyes had been covered with some type of darkened garment or blindfold. She could feel her wrist being bound together, and the person that was doing it was abnormally strong. But she couldn't open her eyes. Not even when her body had harshly made contact with the roughened asphalt after being violently yanked from the car by her legs.

Liz screamed, "Help! Help Meee! Somebody Please!" Liz hoarsely bellowed out in an extremely muffled tone. She felt nothing but hands and feet making contact with multiple parts of her anatomy until soreness had fully consumed her entire upper body from waist to head.

Liz submitted to the pain, but still didn't pass out; something she'd desperately wanted to do since this fiasco had begun.

Was God punishing me for my disobedience? Was He finally trying to teach me a lesson for all of the low down and evil things that I currently tried doing to Talent. Or was it all just a really bad dream. And if so, why couldn't I wake up! Liz worriedly questioned herself.

Liz was fading in and out of consciousness as God's angel could be heard inaudibly whispering something from somewhere in the distance.

But why did God's angel sound like my grandmother, Mrs. B. Lee? Liz confusingly asked herself.

She earnestly prayed to God for the very first time in Lord knows how long, as Mrs. B. Lee finally came to Liz's rescue, discharging a shot into the air from Grandma Clifton's shotgun. The sound of the gun instantly chased away the three assailants that had been whooping Liz's behind for real.

Check! Talent softly whispered to herself, while watching the entire scene unfold from the metal, cushioned-covered, rocking chair that Grandma Clifton loved so very much, as she whistled a familiar tune that blended in perfectly with the seasoned chair's distinguishably loud squeaking.

Talent was loving how a good plan could come together in the blink of an eye, or from something as simple as the snap of a finger.

And the best was yet to come…

Chapter 32

Liz gazed into the shattered glass that sat on her bedroom dresser, desperately seeking certain parts of the mirror that was clear enough for her in order to visibly see the full accuracy of her appearance. The person that was staring back at her, reminded her of some kind of circus freak. The broken glass vividly played tricks on her psyche by enhancing every scar, scratch, bruise, or protruding knot ten times worse than what they actually were.

This instantly caused Liz to renege on the previous promise that she'd just recently made to God only a few short moments before. She knew that breaking her vow to God would eventually lead to even more trouble for Liz over time. But Liz hoped that God would someday forgive her for this as well.

Afterall, the Bible did clearly state in 2nd Chronicles, chapter 7 verse 14, that *if His people, who are called by His name, would humble themselves and pray, and seek His face, and turn from their wicked ways, that He would hear them from Heaven, and forgive them their sin.*

And that's exactly what Liz was hoping and counting on God to do for her, she irrationally thought. There was no way on earth that she would ever rest until she found out who was responsible for attacking her. "Even if my life depended on it," Liz seriously stated into the mangled mirror.

She angrily applied witch hazel to a few of her most hideous scars because certain scars Liz desperately wanted to keep for her own personal reasons.

She blamed Shica, Sheena, and Talent for her current predicament, not giving a second thought as to if any of it was actually true. As long as it was a possibility, then in Liz's mind, that was more than enough for her to gladly wage War!

She instantly grabbed her chrome-plated brass knuckles and box-cutter off the dresser before maniacally exiting her mother's home. Looking for neither of them in any specific order, she steadily searched for them all the same. She hoped that she would run upon Talent first though, if Liz were to be truthful.

Chapter 33

Sunday morning was in full bloom, and Holy Ghost Church of Truth was packed. Grandma Clifton, and her good friend Dean, pleasantly ushered individuals up and down the aisles to help find them seats.

Church hats were everywhere! And I do mean everywhere! They were all different shapes, forms, and sizes; from big to small. In no particular order. The hats made it impossible for some of the people behind them to see, and best believe that there were complaints.

Majority of the women who just so happened to hear the constant mumbling and grumbling, did little, to almost anything to help appease the complainants. Others merely straightened out their so-called dignified shoulders while extending their necks upward even further to its highest positions making it even more difficult for the people behind them to see the pulpit.

Attitudes were flaring up all over the place, and gossip followed closely behind. Most would agree that the choir's singing, and Pastor London's sermon of the day, was definitely needed at the moment.

Potential rampantly bounced from pew to pew with a hidden agenda of his own. He was sneaking back and forth downstairs to the church's kitchen, where he borrowed, not stole, multiple handfuls of those generic chocolate and vanilla duplex Oreo cookies. He started to sell them to each and every kid whose parents or grandparents had already given them their quarters, dimes, and nickels; solely intended for the collection plate.

Big John watched his grandson's every move with pride, nudging Survivor to bring her up to speed on what was going on. He kept her in her seat when she attempted to get up and go put an end to her son's mischievous ways. Big John promised her he would later chastise Potential for his indiscretions, if he didn't forget that is.

You had to admire the young man's tenacity, Big John proudly thought to himself. He nudged Survivor once again so she could continue to acknowledge her son getting his hustle on all throughout the church, leaving him with a pocket full of money, dollar bills included.

She laughed, shaking her head in astonishment, relishing in the fact that her child finally seemed to be getting back to his natural, jovial self. A sight Survivor definitely loved.

Potential wasn't a bad child. Truth of the matter, and most people would admit, he wasn't bad at all. But he was definitely much smarter than kids his age. The shooting incident that he'd survived had only magnified his intellect even more. Something most adults couldn't possibly seem to understand or familiarize with.

To the much older gentlemen of the church, Potential's quick-witted responses, or highly intelligent come backs towards their so-called slick, old-school jargon was considered *sassing*, maybe even being *mannish*, as some liked to call it at times. But that was never truly the case at all. But somehow it was still more than enough to land him into trouble. Sometimes even getting him popped on many different occasions. In those moments, the older gentlemen would sometimes gladly watch, laughing and mimicking the angry expressions of Potential's face, while enjoying their victory.

But it wouldn't stop there.

Potential was a master prankster himself, and no one or nowhere was off limits. Not even the church. Nor the men that frequented it.

Especially not brother "Snookie" Anthony, or Big Mack Horton. They were two of Holy Ghost Church of Truth most devout and loyal deacons that constantly terrorized Potential in the most playful of ways almost every single time that the church doors opened. But they were in return also terrorized back by Potential as well.

Like the time when Big Mack had almost taken Sister Horton out one Wednesday afternoon during the peak of Bible study after being awakened by the constant feel of something crawling up and down his ashy ankles. He suddenly jumped to his feet kicking, swinging, and hollering like a madman sending sister Horton's feathered head-dressing whisking clean to the other side of the room. And Brother "Snookie" Anthony, basically dislocated both shoulders while trying to football tackle Big Mack to the ground.

Big Mack believed that it was all Potential's fault. He could see Potential quietly sitting back, softly snickering underneath his breath after dropping the loosened feather from his hand. The very same piece of material that had fallen from

Sister Horton's hat shortly before Bible study had begun.

Big Mack struggled getting back to his feet after finally breaking free of Brother "Snookie" Anthony's strong embrace. He aggressively yelled at Potential, while trying not to curse. "Why you little! It was you wasn't it! Wasn't It!" He steadily pointed his finger in Potential's direction the entire time.

Potential, yet again, disrupted another incredible service due to his nemesis. He quickly dashed behind Sister Horton, feigning as if he was really afraid. Sister Horton threateningly barked back at her husband in Potential's defense, shielding him with the roundness of her robust frame. From behind her, Potential secretly poked out his tongue.

I oughta' be ashamed of myself, Potential snickered at the fond memory. *But I'm not!* he laughed.

He scoured the congregation until his eyes were once again fixated on the ashy-ness of Big Mack's ankles, who for the thousandth time didn't appear to have on any socks. He rhythmically tapped his foot up and down leaving a huge puddle of dry skin underneath the sole of his shoe.

He was gladly sharing particles of his DNA with the rest of Pastor London's entire flock, whether they wanted him to, or not.

Enthralled with the soulful singing of Holy Ghost Church of Truth's choir, Big Mack never noticed Potential making his move. But, in the midst of doing so, Potential's attention landed on the back of someone's head that he would never ever forget for as long as he lived.

That someone was Officer Long! Potential angrily scowled watching him excessively close.

Officer Long quickly darted out of the church house doors and into a gray sedan where he kindly greeted "The Occupant" with a deceptive grin.

Chapter 34

Sunday services were finally over, and it was now feeding time within the Clifton home. Stomachs churned all throughout the house as all of the smaller children were quickly ushered outside to play, while the adults finished preparing the table and preheating the food.

Although it was a typical Sunday afternoon, it reminded you of the holidays due to the different varieties of food. Mouth's watered, and hands were repeatedly smacked for trying to sneak a quick taste of whatever was available when they figured that no one was looking. Even after the hand smacking, they were handed a little something there afterwards because that's just what family do.

Everything was present from collards to turnip greens. Some cooked with turkey some cooked with pork. Chicken and dressing, macaroni-n-cheese, sweet potatoes, deviled eggs, fried chicken and pork chops. Along with an extremely large selection of homemade pies, cakes, and banana puddings, all made from scratch.

The meal was topped off with some of Grandma Clifton's famous hot-water cornbread. Survivor was the only other person who truly mastered making it. Piece after piece vanished from the hot, cast-iron, skillet no matter how unbearable the grease was. Survivor side-eyeing several of her relatives, giggling as the scorching hot bread burned the roof of their mouth and tongues. But they all still sneakily chewed, tickling Survivor even more.

Witnessing the entire scene unfold right before his very own eyes, Potential stealthily traveled from front to back, until finally making eye contact with someone that was inside. He hoped that he too could also get a few pieces of Grandma Clifton's hot-water cornbread. His plan was to split it with Talent and the rest of his relatives so that the grumbling that existed within their stomachs could also be appeased.

Potential lightly tapped on the back screen door, but never attempted to open it. Magically, a hand appeared. Holding within its grasp were three crispy, golden-colored pieces of bread that were still extremely hot. Potential quickly darted back to the front of the house to split the spoils.

Always one to be teased for not properly chewing his food, Potential devoured the stolen fragments in record time. Afterwards, he remained remotely still for a moment or two longer, realizing that almost any unnecessary movements made on his behalf would possibly vanquish the small portion of food that he had just consumed. That was something Potential did not want.

As he suddenly stretched his small frame out on the hard, metal, cushioned-covered porch swing, he could see a grey sedan parked slightly up the hill from the Clifton home, on the opposite side of the street, and he wondered to himself who that could be.

Chapter 35

The grey sedan was parked up the hill on the opposite side of the street. But neither "The Occupant," nor Officer Long, were in it. The disguise that "The Occupant" had previously chosen for this very special occasion allowed them to blend in perfectly with the current vagabonds of West Nashville. This gave "The Occupant" an opportunity to see directly inside the Clifton's home where the hands of each participating family member were lovingly clasped together in prayer. All except for Liz.

"The Occupant" witnessed Liz standing outside of the bathroom door, glowering as the family prayed. They once again passed the extremely foul-tasting substance they possessed to another newly found associate, whom they were secretly trying to siphon information out of as well.

"This is going to be easier than I thought," The Occupant" said, totally disregarding the dreadful feeling that had suddenly presented itself within the pit of their stomach as a warning sign to retreat. Instead, they steadily blamed it on the disgusting fluids that they were constantly consuming at the time, never once actually realizing that they were being drugged and most likely set up to be robbed by Tank and Cory.

They were two brothers, who in the wee hours of that morning, had secretly witnessed "The Occupant" silently slither from their vehicle, and hurriedly change clothes in between the apartment buildings, where they discarded the garments deep inside a trash bin that sat on the tip of the alley on 32nd Ave. An extremely dangerous place, where in some shape, form, or fashion, almost everyone was connected to the Clifton's.

The loud screams and desperate pleads for help could be heard from blocks away. Begging and bargaining with God, while Tank and Cory administered punishment with no conscience. They knew that "The Occupant" pretty much had those very same intentions for their target in mind as well.

Never once breaking eye contact with "The Occupant," they both delivered some life changing blows, even through the heightened screams of their sorrowful pleas.

"I'm sorry Lord! Please! I'm for real this time!" "The Occupant" sadly begged.

They fell to their knees and tightly closed their eyes in hopes of not receiving another blow while continuously sobbing like a child. Tank and Cory abruptly stopped the beating and finally walked away.

They gave "The Occupant" just enough physical attention for them to fully receive their message; never ever come to West Nashville again in hopes of messing with the Clifton's.

Especially if they truly valued their last few remaining breaths that the Lord had blessed them with. Tank and Cory both agreed before returning back to their regularly scheduled program.

Which was always looking out and doing whatever was necessary to protect the neighborhood. This was a pact that everybody within the community had made amongst each other many years ago.

Chapter 36

The dinner table was set, and Big John had recently blessed the food when Talent meticulously began observing Liz's scars from across the table.

Loving the full impact of her very own vindictiveness for the first time in quite a while, she internally grinned from ear to ear. Deviously winking her eye at her big cousin Liz, still never speaking a word.

Acknowledging Talent's wink, and pretty much on the verge of exploding, Liz somehow managed to hold it all together. Her calmness shocked Talent and she quickly made a small mental note of her big cousin's new resolve before simply making readjustments.

It was early, Talent thought.

She knew that she had more than enough time to continue to antagonize Liz, and she more than planned on enjoying every single moment of it.

She openly admired the scar that currently sat underneath Liz's left eye that sort of put you in the mind of a lowercase "T" or some type of weird looking cross.

Thinking to herself, *my big cousin truly needed Jesus in her life at the moment. But so did I.*

Giggling to herself in embarrassment, she tried to replace her guilt with laughter, as Liz's menacing stare completely burned a hole in the side of Talent's skull. In which, Talent openly ignored. She ticked Liz off even more at that point. But even then, Liz remained composed.

She directed her attention to Potential and a few more of their relatives, who appeared to be captivated with Potential's animated story-telling and jokes, so much so that they never even noticed Talent and Liz's little spat. Unbeknownst to either of them, they all had somehow become an extremely intricate part of Liz's newfound scheme.

Especially Potential, Liz grinned. She winked her eye at Talent before stuffing her mouth full of greens.

Liz enjoyed the sullen expression that currently adorned Talent's face, which over time would eventually become worse as the vileness of Liz's plan slowly materialized and began to take route.

"Check!" Liz openly stated to no one in particular as she smiled with the beadiness of her eyes instead of her lips.

Talent fully understood exactly what Liz meant by the word. Talent spitefully watched her cousin stuff her face with even more of Survivor's food.

The only person's food in which she preferred at that moment for her own personal reasons, as she happily got up from the table to go fix her and Potential a special drink.

Liz secretly sprinkled some sort of white, powdery-like substance into Potential's cup before handing it to him, laughing right along with the rest of her relatives as she made her statement.

"Here cousin, I made us a drink. Taste it. Honestly, it's to die for!" Liz sweetly conveyed.

Evilly winking her eye at Talent once again with a devilish grin, as she casually made her exit.

Chapter 37

"Noooo!" Talent screamed at Potential who almost had the cup up to his mouth in an attempt to take a swig. She smacked it clean out of her brother's hand, while spewing juice all over the pants, body, and t- shirts of all surrounding relatives, except for a few.

"Talent! What is wrong with you? Are you crazy?" Potential angrily barked. He tried his best to wipe the juice off his shirt and trousers before it stained but was having no luck.

Murmuring circulated around the table, but none of it was loud enough for Talent to hear due to the fact that she was no longer present. The others began wiping juice from their outfits as well.

Talent stormed throughout the house looking for her cousin, drawing the attention of a few adults. Who, in all actuality, really paid her no mind.

The audacity of Liz trying to hurt her little brother because of her was an extremely evil move.

One that Liz would most definitely pay for once Talent found her. Talent burst through the living room door which landed her outside where she angrily yelled Liz's name.

She never once noticed her cousin crouched down on the side of the porch, patiently waiting for Talent to exit the house.

She savagely swung the box-cutter with all of her might, and it tore clean through some part of Talent's body according to the ripping sounds of her fabrics.

She tried desperately in her heart to slice Talent's face wide open from cheek to chin or possibly lower before Liz quickly ran away.

Chapter 38

Meanwhile on the other side of town...

There was an extreme awkwardness in the air. Although the sky was clear and the clouds were immensely white, there still appeared to be a certain type of gloom presently surrounding the McCreary home. An unusual oddity that even the McCreary's early morning prayers, or meditations couldn't seem to remove.

Something was amiss. Something that neither Mrs. Ida B. nor T. Thomas, could quite put their finger on. But, yet and still, there it was. A feeling within each of their gut that constantly kept urging the McCreary's that something was wrong.

But what was it? They questioned.

They each steadily tried to keep their composure and not become too overwhelmed because of their paranoia. Mrs. Ida B. lightly tapped on Dorothy's bedroom door before entering. She came to the conclusion that she was no longer there. Which, as of lately, wasn't really much of a surprise, to Mrs. Ida B.

She slowly eased her daughter's door back to a close before making her way to the bathroom so that she could finally finish getting herself together for the scheduled appointment that they both had with Dr. Wiseman. One of which both McCreary's was truly hoping to be their last.

Thoroughly checking all of their appliances before exiting, nothing at all seemed out of place. But the eeriness remained, as T. Thomas double-checked all locks and windows of his home before respectfully leading his wife to the passenger side door of their vehicle.

They both totally disregarded the suspicious looking delivery guy that just so happened to be watching their every move as they pulled away.

Officer Long's ex-partner tailed the McCreary's all the way to Dr. Wiseman's workplace. He instantly was taken back to his undercover days as an officer, where he blended in perfectly with the rest of Meharry's constant influx of cars, utility trucks, and emergency vehicles. He even waved to the McCreary's as he leapt from the truck with materials in hand.

The ex-partner stopped to take a sip of water from the hallway water-fountain in order to allow the McCreary's to pass. He steadily watched over his shoulder as Dr. Wiseman greeted them at the receptionist desk with a smile, before ushering them inside his office.

Once the coast was clear, the ex-partner entered the office as well.

"Hello ma'am. I have a certified letter for a uummmm, Dr. Wiseman, I believe it is," the ex-partner stated appearing to be somewhat unsure as he constantly shuffled through the bogus documents that contained the addresses of several different abandoned properties in that area, before finally finding what it was that he was actually looking for.

"Got it!" The ex-partner exclaimed.

After receiving her signature, he handed the receptionist the letter before saying his goodbye. He quickly stopped at the nearest payphone shortly afterwards to place a call to an individual who answered even before the completion of the first ring.

"It's done," was the only words that were spoken into the receiver before the line went dead on the other end. This left the ex-partner somewhat dumbfounded from the rude non-response as he shrugged his shoulders. "Well, thank you too buddy!" he said.

He hung up the phone before heading back to the delivery truck in order to finally finish off his route. He had no earthly idea that he'd just become an accomplice in a crime, right along with "The Occupant" and Officer Long who were now currently holding Dorothy against her will in the soiled basement of some foreclosed property somewhere deep in the woods.

The place was far away from civilization, where neighbors couldn't hear your screams even if you actually tried. There were honestly no neighbors around.

The basement was filled with all sorts of weird-looking objects. Objects that "The Occupant" had collected from many different foreign countries throughout the world. But the most hideous, medieval-looking objects that "The Occupant" had acquired, were purchased on American soil.

From older surgeons such as their mentor/foster-father. One of the best ophthalmologists that the world had ever seen, from "The Occupant's" perspective. But also one who could no longer legally practice medicine anymore due to the massive heart-attack that they had suffered on behalf of Dr. Wiseman and the McCreary's. "Because of that, they would all have to pay!" the Occupant vowed.

Aggressively unsheathing one of the most diabolical looking blades that Dorothy had ever seen. One that "The Occupant" had specifically purposed for this very moment.

Dorothy's eyes widened with fear, as "The Occupant" slightly pricked certain parts of her body. Becoming more and more animated from the sight of her blood as "The Occupant" quickly entered into character by changing their voice to that of a Distinguished Englishman, using proper pronunciation while quoting Leviticus 24, verses 19-20.

"If a man causes disfigurement of his neighbor, as he has done, so shall it be done to him. Fracture for fracture, eye for eye, tooth for tooth; as he has caused disfigurement of a man, so shall it be done to him," The Occupant calmly stated.

He circled the circumference of Dorothy's resplendent eyes with the extremely sharpened object, never once breaking eye contact with her as he tasted her blood. All the while, seriously contemplating which one should actually be sent to her parents.

"Bone of my bone, flesh of my flesh, and blood of my blood," The Occupant verbalized to Dorothy. They slowly removed their disguise so that she could get a better look at who was standing before her.

Dorothy's eyes almost popped from their sockets while staring at the stranger. She instantly noticed the striking resemblance, as she looked them up and down several times over. It made her sick to her stomach as "The Occupant" allowed her to take it all in for a moment, before finally taking her life.

"Who... Who... Who are you?" Dorothy stammered.

And, without the slightest bit of hesitation, The Occupant viciously answered. "I'm the child that no one wanted! The one that your so-called sanctified parents banished in order to protect the family name! I'm the one that was discarded like trash on the steps of an abandoned church! And the one who's been abused since the day I was born while you were treated like ROYALTY!" they screamed.

"Who am I? I'm your brother Daniel. The one that's going to gladly punish each and every one of you for your past discretions. I'm the one that the whole entire world will forever remember as "The Occupant!" he said.

"And so will you!" The Occupant finalized as he violently swung the blade. He was loving the whistling sound that was mixed in with Dorothy's screams which combined was more like music to "The Occupant's" ears, as he swayed from side to side as if he was actually dancing.

Twirling around in circles now, he sampled a little bit more of his sister's blood, hysterically laughing the entire time...

"Aaaahhh hahahaha! Aaaaahhh hahahaaha!

Chapter 39

"Here Dr. Wiseman, a letter came for you." The receptionist stated totally ignoring the small, red spectacles that completely covered the entire front of the letter as if it didn't exist. She smiled at the McCreary's before once again dropping her head.

Dr. Wiseman skeptically observed the strange letter with no return address but didn't want to seem paranoid in front of his clients.

But his nerves were completely shot!

Reaching for the letter-opener, something told him not to open it. Especially in the presence of the McCreary's.

But he did.

What he read almost stopped his heart from beating. He released the letter and it fell slowly from his hand.

"Dr. Wiseman are you okay? Dr. Wiseman? Answer me honey, you're scaring me!" Mrs. Ida B.

stated. She gently shook his shoulders, trying to draw him back to reality.

T. Thomas picked the letter up and read it. He let out a horrific scream.

"NOOOOOOOOOOO! Not my baby, Lord... Please!" T. Thomas sobbed, falling to his knees, as the words of the letter could be visibly seen by everyone that was currently present.

Dorothy's Gone...
And Y'all R Next!
Truly Yours,
The Occupant!